The slide of Greg____ around the small of her back caused Chris to breathe out in a rush

Using it as a pulley, he drew her forward toward him. Her knees met the couch he was sitting on. Thank goodness for the couch—something solid to keep her knees from hitting the floor.

Greg gave a quick yank and she felt herself falling, guided by his hands on her waist, until she was spilled over him. Their faces so close, her halting gasps fanned his lips. The taste of danger, his voice gritty, challenging and...amused?

"What did you think I was going to do?"

"I didn't know."

"Were you curious?" When she nodded he said, "Curious. That's good. What about...excited?"

Answering honestly, she said, "I was."

"Excellent." He led her hands from his shoulders to the first button of his shirt. "Anything and everything you can possibly imagine...*I want.*"

Dear Reader,

Some of you are old friends, faithful readers who know me as Olivia Rupprecht, romance author. Others of you are new friends; we met once before in my first Mallory Rush Temptation novel, *Love Slave*. As for the rest of you, I hope we can become friends, as well.

Friends. This is how I think of my readers. After all, we have so much in common. Most of us are women who are spread thin, demands from jobs and families leaving us precious little time for ourselves. It's often a matter of stealing it in the bathtub or after everyone else is asleep.

Escape. Who doesn't need it? I sure do. Ah, romance, take me away. I want to feel pretty, I want to relive the first flush of falling in love. And I want to feel sexy. These are wondrous things that make us feel *alive*.

Welcome to *Love Game*. This book is very special to me, and I wish I could say it's for everyone. It is not.

Readers, beware. There is a level of eroticism and a bit of frank language that some of you might take exception to. But for those who, like myself, have longed for a story that blends sexual fantasies with tender emotion and a sweeping romance...

Well, let's just say my publisher and I are eager to hear what you think. Did you enjoy this book? Would you want to read more books like this? Write to me c/o Harlequin Books, Editorial Department, 225 Duncan Mill Road, Don Mills, Ontario, Canada M3B 3K9.

Wishing you happiness and love.

Your friend,

Mallory Rush

MALLORY RUSH

Love

GAME

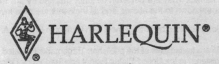

HARLEQUIN®

TORONTO • NEW YORK • LONDON
AMSTERDAM • PARIS • SYDNEY • HAMBURG
STOCKHOLM • ATHENS • TOKYO • MILAN • MADRID
PRAGUE • WARSAW • BUDAPEST • AUCKLAND

ISBN 0-373-83313-X

LOVE GAME

PROLOGUE

"Stop that! Did you hear—Mark! Stop it, Mark, that—that tickles!" Her knees hitched over his shoulders, Chris used her heels to pound his back in time with her squeals of laughter. A playful shove at his head dislodged a fluffy red-and-white cap that skittered beneath the Christmas tree. With a firm clamp on the legs she'd squeezed shut, he spread them and nipped an interior thigh.

"Ho, ho, ho," her equally naked lover replied. "Quit squirming, Chris, and let me give you a hickey."

"No hickey! No hickey, please..." Amid wiggles and giggles and pleas for mercy, Chris tumbled them off their secondhand couch. Rolling over the creaky wood floor, she reached for a long candy cane and smacked him with it.

"Ouch!" Sitting atop her hips, Mark rubbed his jaw.

"Did I hurt you?" Suddenly still beneath him, she touched his mouth—which curled into a suggestive half smile.

"I'm in agony." He bit softly into the heel of her palm, then leaned over her, all playfulness gone. Sifting through the tangle of her hair, he took a dark strand and teased it over her lips. "You love me."

"I love you too much," she answered truthfully. "Mark, I don't think I could live if I ever lost you."

"Then don't think it. You're stuck with me for life."

She drew his mouth to hers. They kissed with tender emotion until their lovemaking escalated and he impulsively pushed into her. Then quickly, he began to pull out.

"No, please no," she whispered, gripping him. "Please, Mark. I want a baby. Your baby, my baby. *Ours.*"

"Chris." His gaze was steady, wise, patient. That was Mark, CPA, MBA, wing tips shiny and conservative suits Martinized clean. He was her rock. "We've only been married two years. We just signed our lives away on a mortgage and we'll be needing a new car before we can—"

"Start a college fund," she finished by rote. Mark was right, she knew. They were young, their future bright. That was logical, and the almost-frantic instinct to conceive that had been in her for the past year wasn't. But there it was. "We can get by. So what if we can't afford formula, I want to nurse our babies anyway. As for clothes, I'd rather sew with remnants than have ready-made."

"Anyone ever tell you that you sound like a home-ec teacher?" He squeezed her hand, gentling the brewing storm. "A foxy home-ec teacher who's married to a guy with a cash register for a brain. At least, that's what you said the last time we got into this."

Turning her head to the side, Chris stared at the slim pile of presents under the scraggly pine they'd cut from her parents' yard in Dallas and hauled all the way to Lubbock. The tree hadn't cost a penny but had more meaning than a hundred-dollar flocked fir.

A baby would be like Christmas. A present to be unwrapped each day of the year, an ever-changing surprise of life and wonder.

"Money is fine and good," she said quietly. "But a baby doesn't care about anything but being wanted and cherished." She implored him with her eyes while seducing his agreement with the upward tilt of her hips. His gaze locked with hers and they shared a taut silence in this, their battlefield, a place where their allegiance was increasingly torn.

"All right, then. If we have to make a few sacrifices, it won't be at the expense of our marriage. A rift between us just isn't worth it." He took a deep breath and committed himself with a thrust. "You're my life, Chris. No man should ever love a woman as much as I do you."

Good and sure was the rock of his hips. She held tight to the arms anchoring her against the floor, desperate to never let him go. What they had together was too wonderful.

The feel of his body emptying inside her own was a bond they sealed with soul-deep kisses. "No regrets?" she asked, just to be sure.

"No regrets, hon, we'll do fine." They hugged each other with fierce affection. "Maybe next Christmas we'll have more than cookies in the oven."

"You'll still want me, even if I'm tipping the scales?"

"You betcha. At least then you can't outrun me if I want to give you a hickey." His grin got him a pinch on the butt.

"For a numbers kind of guy, you sure know how to make a woman feel like she's in the chips."

"Mmm. What do you say that we open our presents, then take another crack at investing in futures? Once my personal stock's on the rise, I'll put up the liquid assets."

"The bank's open and ready for your deposit, sir."

"Deposits. Much more to my liking than withdrawals are, any day." His hands stretched over hers. Their wedding bands fit snugly between the grooves of interlocked fingers. "Jingle bells, jingle bells. Kiss me and let's make them ring."

The scent of drying pine needles and woodsmoke mingled with their hushed, intimate laughter.

CHAPTER ONE

THE SCENT OF DRYING pine needles and woodsmoke mingled with the sound of family laughter.

Chris opened her eyes and smiled as six-year-old Audrey tore open another package from the mountainous pile of gifts. Most had Audrey's name on them. Chris thought it an awful lot for one little girl when so many other children went without. But Audrey went without in ways, too, and she wasn't overly spoiled. Besides, judging from the beaming faces of her own parents, Anna and Don, they were having as much fun as their only grandchild. And if Rick and Tammy, her brother and his wife, had gone overboard on the gifts, Chris knew their hearts were in the right places.

"Wow, neat! Look, Mama, look at what Uncle Rick and Aunt Tammy gafed me." Bounding from the floor, Audrey rushed to the couch and thrust her newest prized possession at her mother. "Isn't she pretty? She looks just like Aunt Tammy. 'Cept Barbie doesn't have a baby in her tummy."

"That's because Ken's not a stud like me, right, Tammy?"

"Whoa, big boy, that's some real competition. A rubber doll who's not even anatomically correct."

Chris watched her brother pat Tammy's stomach as

they shared a grin. They were an inspiration and one
Chris needed, a reminder of how rich life could be.
It seemed that her own heart's good fortune was
spent, and she couldn't deny that poverty had taken
its toll. Not bad on the outside for thirty-three, but
where it counted, inside, she felt like a woman past
her prime. Washed-up, hollowed out, hanging on to
the fringes of other people's lives to fill up the gaps
in her own. And smiling, always smiling until she
thought her jaw would break from the effort. But for
now, it was easy enough.

"What do you say to Uncle Rick and Aunt Tammy,
Audrey?"

Dutifully, the little girl thanked them, then threw
in two big hugs before she tore into the next foil-
wrapped box.

An hour later Audrey was tucked into the old double bed that Chris had slept in as a child. Audrey was
a good little snuggler, but she couldn't take the place
of a large, comforting body to warm cold toes on.
And she wasn't a listening ear that shared secrets on
a pillow deep into the night. Not for the first time,
Chris wished she'd never had that comfort. Never to
have it was never to miss it.

"Did you have a good Christmas Eve, sugar?"

"It was great, Mama. Super good. Almost, anyway."

"Almost? You mean there was something you
wanted that you didn't get?"

"Uh-huh. But Santa comes tonight so maybe he'll
bring me what I really, really want." Audrey looked
confident.

"And what's that, your two front teeth?"

"Uh-uh. But can't tell or maybe I'll jinx it. Only God knows since I told Him—but He's good at keeping secrets." Audrey's quiet smile was poignantly familiar. The hair belonged to her father too, pale colored, fine textured. Chris stroked it back, and touched him through their child. The soulful, deep brown eyes that blinked away the sandman were the only trait she'd passed on to her daughter. In all else, Audrey was Mark's; even his wisdom was reflected in her maturing baby face.

Please don't grow up, don't ever leave me. I need you too much. Swallowing the words, Chris kissed her—a tender kiss that imparted her desperation to hang on to yesterday while her child was slipping too fast into tomorrow.

Leaving on the night-light, Chris left the room. She paused behind the cracked door and, curious, listened.

"Now I lay me— Aw, shoot, You've probably heard that a jillion times. Besides, You know I'm just sayin' it to get to what I want. Please, God, make Santa bring me a daddy. I want one really bad. All my friends have one and they think they're awful neat. And besides, Mama— Well, she doesn't say so, but I think she's lonesome and she'd like it lots if you sent my real daddy back. But if he's too busy with the other angels the way Mama says he is, I bet she'd be happy with someone nice and funny and—"

Chris moved quickly away. The hall, suddenly too narrow and dark, lent its support as she skated her flattened palm against the wall. Once alone in the bathroom, she turned the lock and slumped against the door. No light. No sound, except for a heart that beat dully in her chest, her ears.

"Were you listening, God?" she whispered sharply. "Is there a goddam chance in hell that You listen to little children? Do they possibly get through when a deaf ear's all You gave me when I was on hands and knees and—" Pressing a tight fist against her mouth, Chris bit into her knuckles.

Stop it, she silently railed. *He's gone.* Gone. And no amount of anger, regret or sorrow would change what was. She had to go on. She had to make everyone believe that she was fine. Then maybe she could convince herself. She had worth; she had purpose. Audrey needed her. The family needed her. Even some of her students needed her.

She needed them to need her. Without them, where would she be? *Who* would she be? Chris knew too well they were her only defense against this bitter woman cursing God in a dark bathroom on Christmas Eve.

"Well, Lord," she muttered, trying to summon a bit more respect. A caustic laugh and she went on, "If I couldn't fool Audrey, I might as well quit trying to fool myself. I *am* lonely. But I've had my slice of the pie, so I don't expect a motherlode of generosity. My little girl is something else. She deserves more than presents to make up for what money can't buy. Audrey wants a daddy. Got an extra, by chance?"

Silence. What had she expected? Jingle bells? A kiss to make them ring? With a snort, Chris flipped on the light and fished a cigarette from her pocket. Despite the cold weather, she opened a window to puff the evidence into the frosty night air. Smoking. Just one of the things she hid from those who loved her and thought they knew her best.

They didn't know her, she just let them think they did. Hell, half the time she wasn't sure if she knew herself. Heel hitched onto the toilet lid, she stared into the starry sky and absently finger-drummed her knee.

Make You a deal. Find Audrey a decent daddy and I'll quit bitching. I'm not asking for love, just so he can love her and support PTA. You know, a good guy who likes kids. He doesn't have to be rich or handsome, but a sense of humor would be nice. A few common interests, not too tough to live with—as in, demanding, macho types need not apply—and, say…mutual respect. That'll do it for me, and I'll try hard not to slip and call him the wrong name at the wrong time.

Chris glanced down to where she'd instinctively tensed. Her fingers inched up and brushed the place she'd ignored so long that she'd begun to wonder if her sexuality had decided to go away and never come back.

While we're on the subject… If You can dig up a daddy for Audrey, even if he's not good in the sack, I'd appreciate it if he could spark a tingle. I'd like to like his kisses. But I'm not greedy, he doesn't even have to give hickeys.

Window closed and cigarette butt flushed, Chris gargled, then made a spot check in the mirror. No smoker's breath and no tears. Except for the stray gray hairs she plucked and a few well-concealed lines, she decided she didn't seem much changed from when she'd left for college in Lubbock: pretty and polite, cheerleader vivacious and an honor-roll listee, just the kind of girl a boy's parents liked to meet. *Groan.*

A convincing smile firmly in place, Chris marched out. Before she reached the den, a knock sounded at the front door.

"I'll get it," she called, wondering which relative it would be. Thank goodness she had met her husband at Texas Tech and he hadn't wanted to move away from his Lubbock roots. Even if it did smell like cow shit when the downwind brought the stockyards home, the outskirts of Dallas were far more cloying. In the Adams clan, smother love went way past doting parents.

Pulling open the door, she pitched her voice low to imitate Santa. "Mer-ry Christ-mas…?"

"Chris? Chris Adams?"

"Yes. Well, no. Chris Nicholson."

The man she stared at stirred a wisp of memory. High school. Her, a freshman, with a major-league crush on a senior. Wanting more than anything to wear his letter jacket. Even better, his high school ring; each wrap of surgical tape to take up the slack would be a band of honor.

Three dates that ended with kisses. On the fourth, ending up in the back seat of his parents' Buick. Half an hour past her curfew, Dad meeting them at the door. The fast boy had proved he was an even faster talker. Apologies made, he'd promised it wouldn't happen again.

It hadn't. He'd moved on. While she spent a month with tears on her pillow after listening to the phone not ring, he'd chosen a girl who put out over one with standards. That's where she'd lost him, both of them knowing he'd have a long wait to get more than kisses, a quick feel and…

A hickey.

She touched her neck. A smile spread from her lips and lit up her eyes.

"Greg Reynolds! I haven't seen you since— Come in, get yourself out of that rain."

"No argument here. And just for the record, I haven't forgotten 'since,' either." He grasped her extended hands and stepped into the warm foyer. His gloves were wet and she felt his shiver beneath.

He let go but the shiver remained in her fingertips. It was from the cold, mostly. But a flash of steamy windows in the back seat of his parents' car caused the shiver to linger.

"You're the last person I expected to see at my old doorstep on Christmas Eve. What *are* you doing here?"

"I was on my way to surprise Mom and Dad when the car I'd rented at the airport had a radiator blow just down your street. Much as I hate to barge in, I was counting on your parents' goodwill toward men. Thought they might let me use their phone."

He doffed a military dress cap. Marine, she thought. A slight recession of his hairline reminded her more than she liked of just how many years had passed since they'd parted. What she did like, however, was that he brushed his hair straight back, not trying to hide time's progress with an overlong front strand draped over a prominent forehead. Several lines were creased there, from laughter and maybe some worry and sorrow.

Altogether, the years had treated him well. His jaw was a little large, but firm, and his chin had a small indentation in the middle, as if a fingertip had been pressed into it. His eyes were flecked with several colors, none taking the lead. His nose had been broken in the interim and, if set, it was not a good job. The thick, sandy hair was clipped close to ears into which she suddenly, vividly remembered whispering, "Greg, no, I can't." He hadn't pushed her to pet him again, but a part of her had wished he'd been more persistent.

A slight clutch in her belly took her by surprise. Glad as she was that her body was miraculously showing some signs of life, Chris was sorry it stemmed from an adolescent crush on a boy who was now a man—a man who was sure to be married or divorced and carrying around a lot of emotional baggage.

And you're not? came a small, nagging voice. Shutting it out, she said brightly, "If your car had to break down I'm glad it was here. Where did you fly in from?"

"D.C. Got assigned to the Pentagon after traipsing the globe to wherever Uncle Sam needed me. Man, is it good to be back stateside. Never knew how much I took for granted until it was gone. Sure does make a body appreciate what they've got the next time around."

"You can say that again." Chris, amazed at how easy it was to talk to him after so many years, decided she wanted to talk some more. "You're welcome to stay for eggnog," she said hopefully. "And I'm sure Rick would love to hear about your pro-football days."

"That should take all of two minutes since I didn't make the final cut." Greg's smile was craggy, a little weary, but just as infectious as she remembered. He had a nice smile, with a touch of something else that wasn't so nice. "I'd like to stay and visit, but it's getting late and I'm eager to surprise the folks. If I could use your phone, I'll give them a call to come get me."

"And spoil your banner entrance at their front door? Hang on while I get my coat. I'll drive you."

"You're sure? I hate to take you away from—"

"Sure I'm sure, and Santa can simply eat her cookies and milk when she gets back. Besides, I'd rather hear more about you than pig out on some sweets I don't need."

She squeezed a waist that looked thinner to him now than it had when she was fifteen. He thought her face slightly drawn, too. But it didn't detract from the wholesome prettiness that had matured into a frank beauty—a beauty he found all the more interesting for the character lines life had crafted.

Watching her as she strode away for her coat, Greg was caught by the way she carried herself. There was a stiffness to her spine he recognized as almost regimental, a bearing that was proud, as if trained not to show any hint of weakness. It could have been the same walk as the men he had once commanded, except for the fluid swish of her hips showcased in black leggings that seemed to have no end.

Chris the Dish was still a dish. Straight toothsome smile, high rosy cheeks, Ivory-soap complexion and a mouth to dream about. The dark hair was shorter—just to her shoulders and she wore it in soft waves.

Too bad she was married. One look at that ring on her finger and he knew there would be no making amends for past mistakes. It ate at him some. Chris had a distinct manner that told him she'd realized her potential admirably well.

"Ready?" Keys in hand, she paused in the entryway, beneath a sprig of mistletoe.

"Not quite." Leaning down, he kissed her. Why the hell he did it, Greg didn't know. But he did it just the same.

CHAPTER TWO

IT WAS ONLY HER CHEEK he kissed. But still, her husband might not appreciate the way he lingered. The hint of cinnamon on her breath and the scent of apples lifting from the hair he impulsively fingered, prompted a quick bite of envy inside him.

Judging from Chris's high color she was either embarrassed or transported with him to another place and time: necking like crazy to make-out music on the car radio until he was ready to say he loved her, anything, if she'd give in. His "Please, let me. I won't hurt you, I promise." And then her grip on his wrist, leading his hand away from her panties.

He was there again and feeling the yank in his groin. It was crazy, insane. A man his age didn't get a hard-on with the turn of a dime. *Married.* Shit, wouldn't you know it.

"Let's go," she said suddenly. Once in the car, he started to give her directions. "No need," she interrupted. "I still know the way by heart."

"But I only took you home to meet my parents that once."

"But I only drove by with my girlfriends to check up on you at least a dozen times. I quit after you dumped me for Tiffany Goodbody. Remember? The bad girl with a good body."

"I remember." Groaning, Greg shook his head. "I'm not proud of the way I treated you, Chris. I was immature and a little too full of myself, putting more stock in scoring with a bimbo than waiting for an extra-special girl. There's more than one thing I'd change if I could turn back the clock."

"Same here." That said, she let it drop.

As they tooled down the rain-slick road, neither spoke. The swish of wipers and the patter of a heavy drizzle seemed louder than it should. Didn't they have anything left to say? Strange, but he felt a loss that they had crossed paths again only to part with a "Thanks for the ride and take care." Then again, maybe they'd run into each other at a checkout stand and wave, or fumble for conversation now that they'd hit another dead-end street. Second verse, same as the first.

Their arms and thighs were separated by a stick shift between bucket seats. He took up a lot of room but the car felt crowded with more than the space their bodies consumed. When she turned on the radio he sensed it was more from a need to fill the silence than to listen to "Carol of the Bells."

"Are you sure it won't be an imposition to leave my car in your parents' driveway until the—"

"Of course not." She slid him a brief smile.

"I hope you don't mind what I did," he offered, turning down the radio. "You know, kissing you in the foyer."

"Mind? Hardly. It was the best Christmas present I've had all night."

"No kidding?" At her nod, he touched her hand, which gripped and ungripped the four on the floor.

"You look great, Chris. Even better than I remember. Who's the lucky guy?"

"His name was Mark, but I wouldn't exactly call him lucky. Thirty years old and he had a heart attack. It happened when he was jogging, trying to work off the love handles he'd picked up behind a desk." She laughed—a brittle sound. "Staying-in-shape heart attack, get it? Life's a real joke. It sure had the last laugh on me."

"I'm sorry, I had no idea."

"Yeah, well, it was a surprise to me, too."

"Recent?"

"Almost four years ago."

Reaching over, he tapped her gold band against the steering wheel. "Four years and you're still wearing a wedding ring?"

Her shrug he took to mean indifference, but the passing streetlights illuminated the strain in her profile.

"I've had trouble letting go." She glanced at him sharply, then returned her attention to the road.

Another two miles and they'd be at his drop-off. Another mile and a half...then, maybe a mile to go. Why did her wedding ring bother him? Why did her loss of weight, the tension in her smile? He'd seen friends die. He'd made plenty of personal sacrifices and they'd aged him, too. But none of that seemed to compare with the emptiness he read in the shuttered gaze of a woman who seemed too old too soon.

"We're here," she said, pointing a red fingernail at the solid-as-they-come ranch house.

Who had she done her nails for? he wondered. That ring declared her still bound to a dead man, so she'd likely painted them for herself. Yeah, women were funny that way, making themselves look pretty on the outside when they didn't feel so pretty in places the eye couldn't see. He saw...a terrible waste. Chris probably wouldn't like what he had to say. Tough, Greg decided. He was saying it anyway.

"I've never gone through your situation, so if I sound insensitive, I don't mean to be. But look, you're plenty young to make a new life for yourself. Seems to me you've hung on to your grief, Chris, that you're still tied to the past. Not to say you need a man to make your life complete, but surely it would be fuller with some company. A wedding ring does *not* spell opportunity for any man who might be interested in getting involved with you."

She said nothing but stared straight ahead. Before his parents peered out the window, he killed the engine and turned off the headlights.

Chris slowly turned to him. Even more slowly she slid a finger down his gloved hand.

"And would you be...interested?" A smile crept to the corners of her lips, then wavered. "I can't believe I said that, Greg. Flirting, I was actually flirting with you!" She laughed self-consciously. "Trying, anyway. It's been so long, I don't even remember how. I'm sure your wife wouldn't like me brushing up my skills on her husband." She paused, waiting for confirmation. He gave her none, wanting a confirmation of his own. "You are married?"

"In a manner of speaking."

"Oh." She summoned a jaunty smile that didn't quite make it. Giving it up, she admitted, "Wouldn't you know, I finally hook up with someone whose company I like and—bummer, he's taken."

"Yes, ma'am, he is. Worse than married, he's sworn to a jealous mistress—the Marines." Greg tipped his hat. "Sorry I set you up but a week's leave doesn't give me much slack for subtlety. I want to see you again."

"For old times' sake?" Even in the dim light he could see the hint of a blush. Oh yeah, she remembered the magic they'd made. Question was, just how open was she to making some more?

"Old times are just that. I'd rather enjoy the present than dwell on the past." He caught the lapels of her coat and pulled her closer. Her willingness to let him kiss her, as he fully intended to do, didn't mesh with the apprehension etched in her face. "I'm sorry you lost your husband but I am glad that you're not spoken for."

"But I am! I mean...I have a little girl, Greg. Audrey, she's six."

Hiding behind her child, was she? Chris, he decided, was actually afraid of a simple kiss. Hard to imagine that, but the last thing he wanted to do was scare her off. Besides, it wouldn't be much of a kiss if she didn't loosen up.

"I'll bet Audrey's a cute kid," he said, easing his grip.

"Darling. She looks just like her dad."

"And every time you look at her, you see him, right?"

"How did you know?"

"Doesn't take an Einstein to read between the lines." He pried free the fingers she'd frozen over the stick shift. A soft kiss to their tips, then he urged her arm around his neck. Even through the layers of her coat, he could feel her shaking. His sympathy mingled with frustration as he watched her left thumb work that damn ring like crazy. "Are you cold?" he asked when her teeth began to chatter.

"Freezing," she confirmed.

"I can't imagine why. After all, there does seem to be four of us in here—a ghost, a daughter, you and me." When she blanched, he paused. The most decent thing he could do would be to send her running. "Hey, what say we have a party, add in a few more guests. Think we can make room for my two ex-wives? And how about my hellion teenager? That should heat things up considerably. Warm yet?"

He was glad her shaking stopped, but regretful he'd surely eat her dust without so much as a goodbye kiss.

"So, you have a teenager. What's her name?"

Hot damn, surprise, surprise. Maybe she was staying to chat, but even hanging out with bad news wasn't smart for a woman as vulnerable as Chris obviously was. Greg studied her, eyes narrowed on her too-soft features.

"Arlene. She's fourteen."

"From your first marriage?"

"If that's what you want to call it. A paper with an unwilling signature does not a real marriage make."

"I see," Chris said with an understanding he hadn't expected. "Even if you weren't happy about it, you did do 'the right thing,' which is more than a lot of boys are willing to do these days."

"At twenty-two, I wasn't exactly a boy. I was old

enough to live up to my responsibilities. Unfortunately, Arlene's mom didn't take hers seriously enough. To be exact, she wanted to get married but I wasn't ready to settle down so she conveniently forgot a few pills.'' When Chris nodded sympathetically, he went on. ''Once it was a done deal, I tried—but I didn't try hard enough. I cheated on my first wife, Chris.'' He touched his nose. ''Frying pan, right between the eyes.''

''She caught you?''

''No, I confessed. I didn't love her but I did have a bad case of the guilts—until that cast-iron skillet cleared my conscience. I told myself she deserved it, that it was her fault I was trapped with a wife and baby I didn't want. Her fault that I didn't make the pro-ball cut because my head wasn't in the game. Because it was her fault that I was already worried about finding a job with a history degree that was fairly useless in the job market.''

''Oh, Greg,'' she said softly, ''you must have been terribly unhappy.''

''Miserable. And misery liking company, I made sure she was just as miserable as me.''

''You mean, you kept cheating to get back at her?''

''That look on your face tells me you're almost as disgusted as you are curious.'' He laughed at her, and then, at himself. ''The hell I ever cheated again. I didn't feel man enough to satisfy one woman, let alone two. The truth is, if I'd really been man enough, I never would have stepped out on her. It was inevitable that we'd split, but after we did I came to terms with where a good part of the blame belonged.''

''And where was that?''

"Right here." He tapped a finger to his chest. "Of course, that didn't keep me from making bigger and better mistakes. After divorce number two, it dawned on me that I make a lousy husband."

"Maybe the third time will be the charm." Greg stared at her red nails as she patted his gloved hand. He wasn't one for playing on a woman's sympathy and the fact Chris's felt so good and welcome was enough to make him wish those nails of hers were clawing his back. That was familiar and safe; this warm-fuzzy something he felt wasn't.

"Won't happen, Chris. Three strikes, you're out. I'm not going back to bat now that I've finally reached a place where I'm satisfied with my life. Living alone suits me. So does having no demands other than my career. If I get lonely sometimes, Arlene comes to visit me every other summer and that's enough to make me appreciate loneliness for company."

"I take it you don't get along."

"It's not so much that as the fact she scares the hell out of me. Arlene is The Teenager from Hell. She's the kind of bait that can't wait to get bit, and all I can do is shake my head from the sidelines. It's where I've been all her life, so, as you might guess, I'm no better in the Daddy department than I am at marriage." *Why was he telling Chris this stuff?* Comfort and conversation were luxuries in his wasteland of a personal life and he had no intentions of developing a taste for what he couldn't have for keeps.

Quickly, he shifted the conversation her way. "You, on the other hand, strike me as a devoted parent. It's my guess you won't have the same problems when Audrey's older.''

"They grow up no matter what, don't they?" Chris sifted her fingers through the hair at his nape, the motion more distracted than intentionally provocative.

"We did, didn't we? Some of us just take longer to grow up than others." The feel of her nails skirting his neck was intensely arousing. He wanted a kiss— a deep, wet kiss—and he wanted it now. Only he didn't get the feeling it would be wholeheartedly returned. Yet. Intimacy—the emotional kind that Chris demanded—was not his forte. But if that's what it took to get the kind of kiss he wanted, well, a man had to do what a man had to do.

"You know, Chris, I'm a very private person. I've told you more tonight than I've let on to friends who have known me for years."

"Then, why me?"

"Oh, I dunno. Maybe because I'm hoping you'll ditch this 'I'm okay, you're okay' attitude that I don't buy for a minute. I'm *not* okay, Chris—unless we're talking professional. I think you know where I'm coming from and that's where I'm trying to connect. Do we?"

"Enough that you're making me feel uncomfortable."

"Nothing wrong with that. Uncomfortable's upfront and personal. And personally, I could use an okay feeling with someone who doesn't have any expectations of me. You?"

Something flickered in her eyes—an eager, hesitant something. "Yes, Greg, I *could* use an okay feeling for a change. I need it so much I'll even return the doubtful favor you're asking for. I'm a mess. A god-awful mess. You're looking at a closet basket-case who can't get her act together. My life—'' Her catching sob tugged at him with a force more startling than the raw pain he saw in her eyes before she turned away. ''My life is so screwed up that I wouldn't mind trading places with you. I mean, you're happy with what you've got, right? I'm not. I hate my life the way it is. I *hate* it.''

''Then why don't you change it?''

''Because… I want to. It's just that I don't know how.''

He had hoped her exposure would tumble some walls and get him the touch he was after, but this was more than he'd bargained for. He felt no pride for his selfish manipulation, but he did feel a keen compassion as he absorbed what he'd laid open.

Drawing her close until she buried her face in his neck, Greg asked gently, ''Want to talk about this?''

''No.'' She caught her breath and took a dry heave. Clasping his shoulders, she pulled away and gave him an overbright smile. ''I'm fine, really. I don't know what got into me. The holidays, I guess. They're always the worst. It's a shame, but I can't wait to get past New Year's Day. Less than a week and I'll be—''

''In no better shape than you are now.'' When her fragile smile crumbled he felt a triumph he didn't take much pleasure in. ''Look, I'm not happy with the life I've got, just satisfied. Sometimes that has to be enough because it's better than nothing. But to get there, a person has to cut their losses and move on.'' Swiveling her wedding ring, he said firmly, ''That's what you have to do, Chris. You've got to get rid of this and move on. I've been lobbying for a kiss like never before, but ain't no way that's gonna happen—not with me or anyone else—until you let go.''

She was silent for a while, staring at her gold band, and then at him. Quietly she said, ''Do you actually think my kissing a man who admits to making a mess of his own life will make mine better?''

''Couldn't hurt. After all, what do you have to lose?''

Too much when I've got nothing as it is. She didn't say it, but she didn't have to. He could do one of the things he did best—find the path of least resistance and get what he wanted—but he didn't. Instead, he waited, trying not to hope too much but hoping too much all the same.

When patience became an awkward lapse of words and movement, he decided to stick with what he did better than best: cut his own personal losses and move on.

''Thanks for the lift. See ya…maybe in another eighteen years?'' As he reached for the door handle, Greg felt her grip on his arm, her nails biting softly through the heavy layers of winter clothing.

''Stay? Please, Greg. Stay.''

He paused, giving her time to reconsider. The concern she dug up inside him made *him* uncomfortable. Whatever was going on between them was…unusual. As for Chris, the safest thing she could do would be to open the damn door and push him out faster than spit could hit ground.

When he didn't move, Chris fought a wave of panic. Why didn't he say something? she wondered.

And then she wondered, *Why didn't she? Say something, do something,* she ordered herself. *For once, take control.*

Adrenaline mixing with the rush of anticipation, she pressed her lips to the back of his neck. Her nuzzle was a decision of forward momentum. Flushed with excitement, she took another step with an exploratory flick of her tongue from behind his ear to the starched rim of his dress shirt.

He tasted of ache. Achingly masculine, a composite of the day's last traces of cologne, the faint salt flavor of skin diluted by the rain that had brought him here. Here, in a closed car where the sounds of their breathing mingled. His, heavy and deep; hers shallow as he turned and opened his coat, inviting her in.

"Not yet." Decisively, she raised her left hand, poised between their faces. The moon's watery light haloed her slow lift of gold. The ring, departing from her finger, felt as fragile as life's precarious balance, and then, like Mark, it was gone. Chris kissed the band she should have parted with long ago. This she well knew, just as she was aware of a worse folly: She had loved Mark too much, and not even he was worth the price she had paid. Never again would she risk such vulnerability; never would she forfeit the autonomy she now claimed. And with that silent vow, she laced tight her heart.

Her heart was where she slipped the ring, between breast and bra. Greg's eyes followed the movement and lingered as she began to rebutton her red silk blouse. Pausing there, she decided to leave it undone, exposing a wisp of white lace.

His brow lifted. So did the side of his mouth.

"I'm impressed." He kissed the satin riding over the swell of her breast. "I'm impressed by this almost as much as I am with what you did. That took some guts, Chris."

"More than guts." She tossed his hat onto the dashboard and savored the freedom she claimed in that small act. Pulling him forward by his tie, her grip ate its length until they were separated by a whisper's distance. "It took you to help me find them." And then her whisper brushed aside the final barrier. "I want to kiss you."

"Then do it."

And do it, she did.

CHAPTER THREE

"CHRIS? HELLO, anybody in there?"

"Huh?" She'd zoned out again, Chris realized. So far, she'd escaped a family inquisition as to why she'd been so late getting back the night before. Much more of this and they'd drive her nuts trying to find out what was up. "Sorry, Tammy, what were you saying?"

"Not much. Just that I'm dying my hair purple next week, Rick's been elected to Congress and Mom's having an affair with Tom Cruise. When you said, 'That's nice,' I figured I'd lost you." Topping off their coffee cups at the breakfast nook where they sat, Tammy asked nonchalantly, "So tell me, how does he kiss? After all, it does give a lot of insight into a man's character. You know, sensitive or aggressive. Both and more if he's a really special kind of guy."

Chris chewed on a doughnut, trying to form an answer—more for herself than Tammy. Greg didn't kiss like he used to, when he'd plowed ahead for a touchdown and dropped the ball where she'd drawn the line. Last night he'd kissed like a man who knew how to get what he wanted from a woman's mouth and savored every inch of ground they covered together. It had been an intensely personal kiss that went beyond the usual lip-to-lip, slip-of-the-tongue, I'm-out-of-here-unless-you-slip-yours-back sort of predictability.

Nothing had been predictable about that kiss. Not the way he spent more time on her neck and in her hair than on her mouth. Not the frank way he spoke about how she tasted—"damn good"—or wanting to know how it made her feel when he teethed her nipple between bra and blouse. Apparently "Dear God" hadn't been answer enough. He'd drawn away then and stroked his chin while she clenched his shirt and gasped for breath. His affectionate peck on the cheek had been the last thing she'd expected. That and his sudden "Let's sleep on this, Chris. Sweet dreams. Merry Christmas and...good night."

"How does he kiss? Tell me and we'll both know," she finally said. "Look, Tammy, I'm a little confused and I'd like your input. But you have to swear to silence."

"Gag order, no problem."

"Not a word, not even to Rick." At Tammy's nod, Chris held up her left hand.

"Your ring! You took off your ring!"

"Mark's dead, Tammy, and he's not coming back. I've known it all along, but I wasn't willing to accept it." Glancing out the window, Chris thought how much clearer the sky looked, how much brighter the sun appeared than it had the morning before. The day was too beautiful to weep over a closed coffin. So much time wasted. But no more. *No more.* "I let my life go stale and I'm disgusted with myself for wallowing in the dregs."

"Wallowing in the dregs?" Tammy repeated.

"How can you say that? You're strong. You've survived."

Chris shook her head. "Going through the motions of living isn't the same as getting on with life. Greg gave me a taste of life last night and now I'm ready to make up for lost time."

"This Greg, he must be a special person."

"He's special but he's not for me—or anyone else—in the long run."

"A confirmed bachelor?"

"Worse! The man's been divorced twice and he's got a teenage daughter who scares the pants off him."

"A lot of parents don't know how to handle their kids when they start demanding their space, so he's not alone there. But the ex-wives? That doesn't sound so good."

An unexpected urge to come to Greg's defense rose up in Chris. But what could she say? That he'd cheated on one wife and after the second marriage didn't pan out he'd realized he made a lousy husband? She'd found herself wondering about those women. Relationships did take two people to make them work, and Greg's willingness to assume the blame did count for something. Didn't it? For some reason, she wanted it to.

"Wives or no wives, he's only here for a week. Then back he goes to Washington to huddle with his fellow warmongers. And back I go to Lubbock. Playing Mommy, teaching school, and keeping my eye out for a decent daddy who won't mind ironing his own shirts and eating take-out Chinese. But before I get sensible, I could use a hot date with a hunk." With a sense of personal victory, she announced,

"I've decided to ask Greg out for New Year's Eve. Cool, huh?"

"Not Greg Reynolds, I hope?" Rick said as he entered the kitchen.

Tammy got up and hugged her husband while Chris busied herself by pouring more coffee, intent on ignoring the earful of advice she was sure to get.

"Reynolds was a hell of a football player, should've made it with the Cowboys. I'm glad you're getting out, but don't forget his reputation for scoring wasn't limited to the playing field. Maybe he's changed. Maybe he hasn't."

"Yes, brother dear," Chris simpered. "But may I remind you that your reputation wasn't any better before Tammy settled you down. So there." She stuck out her tongue at him.

"Cute tongue you've got, sis. Just be sure to keep it in your mouth when he's around or you might not get it back." Rick meowed. "Then again, maybe that's not such a bad idea. You wouldn't have it to lash me with—*ooof!*"

Tammy's punch to his stomach coincided with Chris's fling of a doughnut. She hit her target: his nose.

"PHONE, CHRISSY," Anna called to her daughter. Chris felt her heart speed up and her stomach drop. Forcing herself not to run like a starry-eyed schoolgirl, especially when it was bound to be a relative or a friend or— Who was she kidding? *Please let it be Greg,* she prayed, forgetting she had no faith in prayers. "It's a man," her mother whispered.

Yes! *Yes!* "Hello?" she answered, waving Anna away.

"Merry Christmas, Chris." His voice washed over her and made her feel too good, too young, and all-too-alive. Her palms were wet, her throat was dry. Lord, even her knees were shaking! And her breath—she couldn't catch her breath.

"Greg, hi! I didn't expect to hear from you today."

"I called to find out if the car was picked up."

Her high spirits immediately sank, reminding her of those days once made or broken with a phone call from Greg. It had been a long time since she'd eaten a quart of ice cream to pick herself up after he'd dropped her. "Yes, they came. We had the pickup guys in for a cup of eggnog. Must be a drag to have to work on Christmas Day."

"Yeah, it is. I've done it a time or ten." He chuckled then. "Actually, Chris, the car was just an excuse to call. I've been thinking about you and I wanted to hear your voice."

For a moment her voice was nowhere to be found.

"Chris? You still there?"

"Yes, I—" She laughed at her own foolishness, the delight she took in being foolish for a change. "Know what? I think I've got a crush on you again."

"I know I have one on you. It's a kick, isn't it? At least when it's not being horrible. I've been circling this phone for most of the day, telling myself to be cool and not pick it up because then I'd be very uncool and tell you how much I want to see you again. Guess I'm not as cool as I used to be." And then she heard it. A kiss. A soft, short kiss that sent silver bells ringing. "Anyone ever tell you that you've got a mouth that won't quit?"

She'd been told she was a good kisser but a mouth that wouldn't quit, that wasn't exactly the same. It made her feel, well, *carnal*. Carnal? *Her,* the good widow and hovering mother, *carnal?* It gave her the strangest sensation, like peeking into an open bedroom and witnessing an act of mindless sex. Knowing she should move away but too mesmerized, too aroused by the view to leave. And then, the shocking realization that the woman writhing on the bed was her. She, the intruder merely watching herself from a distance.

"Are you free tomorrow night?" Chris suddenly asked.

"As of now, I am. Can you be ready by seven?"

A vision of Audrey looking Greg up and down, then asking, 'Are you going to be my new daddy?' sent Chris scrambling for an out. "Since you don't have a car I'll pick you up."

"No need. I'll borrow the keys from Dad." Laughing, he added, "Maybe he'll slip me a ten after Mom reminds me not to show off behind the wheel and to be home by midnight."

Moments later Chris stared at the cradled receiver. Apprehension swirled in the pit of her stomach. Excitement, smacking of a delicious, dangerous risk, stole away any desire for dinner. It was an oddly nostalgic moment, reminding her of the horrible, wonderful effect hormones could have on appetite.

She wanted to be alone. Curled up in bed, painting her toenails to the tunes from a classic rock station, nirvana.

"Who was that man calling you?"

Chris managed a stiff shrug for her mother and a casual "Oh, it was just Greg. We're going out tomorrow night. You won't mind watching Audrey, will you? Maybe you could even take her to McDonald's while I'm getting ready." *And please, take the rest of the troop with you. Big Macs all around, my treat. Just don't show your faces until I'm gone.*

"Why, Chrissy, a date with your old boyfriend! Where are you going, honey? Are you nervous, excited—"

"Really, Mom, it's no big deal. Pass the word?" Chris pecked her cheek and headed for the bedroom that still had cheerleading pom-poms tacked next to a high school pennant.

Door closed, she went straight for the closet.

What did she have to wear? Nothing too great. She'd hit a mall first thing in the morning. Her perm was about gone but a fresh one would be too tight. The curling iron would have to do. Fingernails? She could use a manicure....

GREG CHECKED HIS WATCH. Ten minutes early. Should've driven around, checked out the old stompin' ground. Alone. *Jeez, what was he doing here?* Sitting in her driveway—better check his watch again. Tapes, which tape?

Let's see. *The Best of Bread*...Rod Stewart, *Every Picture Tells a Story...Seventy of the 70s Greatest Hits*—better shove that one back in the glove compartment, too nerdy to shell out $7.77 for a Ronco job.

Ah, Michael Bolton's latest. Slip it in...check the

watch— *What the hell was he doing here?* Feeling like some green kid worried about getting a good-night kiss while he worked up the nerve to knock on a door, sling back his front hair and say, coolly of course, "Hi, ready to roll?"

Like he still had the hair to sling back. Checking his image in the rearview mirror, Greg suddenly laughed. *Aw, man, you oughta be sweatin' bullets. What'd you think this was, a date for dinner? Uh-huh, sure. That's why you flipped a coin when you couldn't decide between white briefs and black boxers.*

Poor Chris. He never should have called her, never should have kissed her. That kiss, it wasn't just a kiss, and he had no business messing with a woman who put so much gut emotion into a kiss.

Leaning back, he considered that kiss, the reason he was really here. Simple. She'd been needy and he'd eaten it up.

Long time since he'd felt needed for more than balls on a battlefield—be it for country or in a bed. Well, he slept alone mostly. What with being a little needy himself, recreational sex just didn't cut it anymore. Pity he'd lost his appetite for it—about the time his hair began its slow but noticeable retreat. Funny, he thought, how a man's priorities could rearrange themselves when his body started doing the same.

Sex. He loved it. The sounds, the smell of it, the way a woman tasted, how she looked when she came. The sweat, the fit, even the awkwardness of trying to find the right fit with an unfamiliar body. But screwing, it wasn't enough anymore. He wanted a woman with character, class, lots of nooks and crannies upstairs. Someone who knew how to laugh and live for the moment because tomorrow was tomorrow and demands weren't part of the bargain.

Poor Chris. She deserved better than the best he had to offer. Damn, but he wished that he didn't like her; even worse, he respected her. She was the kind of woman who would win a whistle and keep walking without so much as a turn of her head. Bad luck— she'd turned his.

Getting out of the sedan, Greg leaned against the door and waited for the cold air to work against nature. Amazing that Chris could still do it to him at his age. Then again, maybe not. From what he'd seen so far, she was like a vintage wine: the blush, a deeper shade of pale; the crisp flavor, more mellow and rich; a bouquet that was meant to be savored.

Yeah, she'd go down easy.

"STAY PUT, I'LL GET IT!" Purse in hand, Chris rushed to the door on ready. And then she wasn't ready at all.

She'd always felt creepy about men who looked a woman up and down—but judging from Greg's lazy smile, he didn't mind a bit when she surveyed him. Two nights ago he'd looked good, even plane-rumpled and tired. But freshly shaven and dressed in a soft white sweater with pressed jeans, Greg was *mur*-der. The bushy poinsettia with a fat red bow and the easy confidence of his stance as he held it out proved the real killer.

Dying had never been so sweet.

"Why, Greg, how thoughtful of you."

"Think your mother will like it?" She hadn't

planned on inviting him in, but in he came anyway. "It's a little thank-you to your folks for lending me their driveway and a big suck-up in advance—just in case I get you home past curfew."

Chris set the plant on the hall table and was trying to figure out how to make them scarce without seeming rude when Rick made his entrance.

"Hey, Greg Reynolds, good to see you." The two men shook hands and she noticed it lasted longer and they gripped harder than a friendly greeting would dictate. "Chris says you're one of a few good men these days. What's your rank?"

Chris gritted her teeth. Credentials, intentions, warnings with a handshake. Less than a minute and Greg was getting grilled before they could take off for a simple date.

"Major, as of last month. You're Rick, right?"

"That's me. You've come a long way since skirmishes on the twenty-yard line. Chris says you've been assigned to the Pentagon. That's quite a coup, isn't it?"

"I guess you could say so. But like anything else, it's a matter of what you want and how much you're willing to sacrifice to get it. I've paid my dues, proved myself in active duty. Once I did that they caught on where I really belonged was behind a desk. Go figure."

"Must be boring to shuffle paper after seeing that kind of action."

"Top secret, Rick, so my agenda's not exactly boring. I still get around."

"I'm sure you do."

Chris grimaced. *Oh, this was embarrassing, ridiculous. The only thing worse would be—*

"Hi! I'm Audrey. Who are you?"

"So, you're Audrey." Greg bent down and formally shook the small hand that disappeared in his. "I'm very pleased to meet you, young lady. Call me Greg. I'm an old friend of your mom's. Maybe we can be friends, too."

"Neat. Want to come with me and Grandma to McDonald's?"

"I'd like that, but maybe another time. Your mother and I are eating out at a competitor's—"

"A what?"

"A com—somewhere besides McDonald's." As if realizing he wasn't speaking her language and wasn't sure if he could, Greg rose. He towered over the child Chris suddenly wanted to whisk away. A suitable father he wasn't, and she felt a nudge from her conscience for wanting to be with him instead of with a daughter who was counting on Mama's good judgment.

"Tell you what, Audrey. Since you're loaning me your mother for the evening, I'll bring her back with a surprise to put under your pillow. What's it to be? Candy?"

"I'm tired of candy."

"Then, maybe a present?"

"Nope. Do you believe in Santa Claus?"

"Uh, sure."

"Do you like kids?"

Scooping Audrey into her arms, Chris gave her a fierce hug. "Mind your grandmother or the only surprise you'll get is a piece of coal."

"You're squishing me, Mama!"

Chris put her down and tossed a withering glare at Rick. She grabbed the coat she'd conveniently hooked by the door. Greg took it and spread the lining. One arm was in when she heard her parents' voices close by.

"Let's go, Greg," she said abruptly.

Chris bolted for the exit. She didn't say goodbye.

CHAPTER FOUR

"GREAT RIBS," GREG pronounced. "Only place to compete is Kansas City. But I'll take Dallas any day, just so you're here."

"I'm glad I'm here. You're good company, Greg. Sorry about Rick."

"Don't be. He was looking out for his sister and I give him credit for that." Leaning closer, Greg said in a private tone, "If it was anyone but you, I would've ordered a steak instead of the ribs I wanted. They're a little too messy to impress someone you don't know too well on a date. By the way, you've got sauce on your upper lip." When she reached for her napkin, he caught her hand. "Funny, I never realized barbecue sauce could look sexy on a woman."

The air fairly hummed with an illicit vibrato that shut out the voices surrounding them, and she thought he was going to kiss her at last. Eyes half-closed and lips parted, Chris felt the glide of his wet fingertip wiping away the last traces of sauce. Then his finger was no longer there but at his own mouth where he discreetly sucked the remains.

Somehow, that seemed a lot more intimate than a kiss.

"Dessert?" he asked politely.

Two bites of pecan pie was all she could get down

and he finished what she couldn't. Rather than seeming rude or overfamiliar, his use of her fork, his sharing the same plate, rivaled his finger kiss of the sauce. Those liberties were subtle but telling, as was his prudently generous tip, his slide of her chair and "Ladies first" as he held open the restaurant door. Altogether, they heightened her desire for the kiss so much that Chris considered stopping him and *taking* what she wanted.

She couldn't bring herself to do it. Old habits died hard.

"You're hobbling. New shoes?" he asked, slowing his pace.

"Half a size too small but they looked so good, I couldn't resist. This is absolutely *the* last time I buy for appearance instead of the right fit."

"Sounds like me and marriage." He laughed, making himself the butt of the joke. Chris thought it a rare ability and an immensely appealing trait.

"I could learn from you, Greg."

"How's that?"

"You don't let life beat you down by taking it too seriously."

"Don't be so sure." He stopped her with a firm clamp on her waist, a narrowing of his eyes that spelled *t-r-o-u-b-l-e.* Suddenly, her feet left the ground and she was in his arms laughing with abandon as he growled ferociously against her neck. She yelped when he threw her in the air, catching her just when she was certain she'd been dropped.

"Put me down!" she shrieked, not caring about onlookers or reputation, simply cutting loose, not giving a damn, for once— Oh, when had she had this much fun?

"Wanna race me to the car?"

"I'll be a cripple before I get there!"

"In that case, enjoy the ride." His easy shift of her weight over his shoulder amazed her a little. A young athlete's firm muscle could go to flab by the time he was eyeing forty. It seemed that Greg had avoided the pitfalls of comfort the same way she sidestepped even the hint of a conflict. But watching the way his legs moved, two trunks of equal sureness and strength, attached to the tempting view of tight buttocks, Chris decided a conflict might not be so bad after all. She swatted his backside.

He swatted hers back. "You've got a great ass," he said conversationally, and then he bit it. "Betcha taste even better without your clothes. Ah, here we are."

He tumbled her into the car. On his side.

Her first instinct was to scoot to the opposite door—a generous length in a luxury sedan—and think about the last half-minute. Compromising on her sudden cowardice, Chris opted for the middle and put her purse between them.

Greg cranked the engine, hit the tape and pitched her purse into the back seat. He patted the spot beside him.

She inched closer until their hips met. The feel of his arm around her, the slow rub of palm to shoulder, raised gooseflesh beneath her coat.

"Where to?" asked the man who bit butts in parking lots and thought she'd taste better without her clothes.

"Do you like to dance?" she ventured.

"Slow's no problem, but a fast number and I'll trample what's left of your feet."

Did she really suggest *dancing?* A lesson in humility she didn't need. "We could hit a club and have a nightcap."

"Tell you what, if you don't like my idea of a good time once we get there, say so and we'll catch whatever's playing on the big screen, then top off the night with a drink."

With a calmness she wasn't feeling, Chris agreed to his small intrigue. There was an edge of purpose she sensed in him and it felt more darkly suggestive than a kiss. By the time he drove into a deserted shopping center, her palms were pumping sweat. When she began to wipe them on her new suede skirt, he quickly placed her hand high on his thigh.

"Your skirt's too nice, wipe your palms on me." The firmness of thick muscle flexed beneath her touch and she was caught between a tingling quiver and chagrin that Greg was aware of her slipping composure.

He circled the parking lot—ensuring they were alone, she suspected—then, once in the back, pulled into a reserved spot.

Off went the car lights but the engine still idled.

"Know where we are?"

"It's familiar but—no, I can't place it."

The brush of his lips was a restrained hunger. Her own hunger mingled with taut nerves and she hoped he'd keep kissing her until the first consumed the other.

"Do you remember now?"

"This is where we used to go parking."

"The concrete walls weren't here, but you had some walls of your own I did my best to crack."

"You made more than a dent." Her smile was a little wobbly; so was her voice. "After all, you gave me my first hickey."

"The most persuasive thing I knew to do with my mouth. *Then*." The engine continued to idle against the innuendo that he wanted more than a repetition of old memories. She'd heard the dating game had changed since she'd been an active player, but it distressed her to think Greg would hold her in such shallow regard.

When Michael Bolton began crooning a new song, Greg switched on the lights. "So what movie do you want to see?"

"Wait." Chris gripped his hand on the shift. "I have to know, did you expect casual sex as payment for dinner?"

"Casual sex?" he repeated, a hint of amusement in the lift of his brow. "Why, Chris, surely you realize any sex we might have would *never* be of the casual variety. And there's certainly not much variety to be had in a car."

"Then what are we doing here?"

"I had hoped," he said slowly, "we might make some good memories to keep us warm when life turns cold." Shifting into reverse, he added, "I'm somewhat offended that you thought I would pressure you for sex because I sprang for the meal. That's not my style and I've yet to take anything from a woman she wasn't more than willing to give."

Truth or dare; Chris twisted the key. The engine

ceased to purr and she imagined he could hear her dry swallow.

"Forget the movie. Unless it's at a drive-in." It was she who turned off the lights, and it was she who said in a trembling whisper, "Wanna make out?"

Determined to forge past her qualms, she closed her eyes and waited. And waited. Until finally, she blurted, "What are you waiting for?"

"You." His lids were lazily drooped over his eyes. "You're tense. Like this is something you're bent on doing because it's good for you, not because it's easy and natural."

"Of course, it's not easy," she retorted, flustered. "And you're certainly not making it any easier for me, staring at me like that, like...like— Ah, hell. Maybe *you* want to take in the last show." Why was he making this so difficult? Scrutinizing her until she couldn't stand it a second longer. She turned away. "I'm not too good at this, Greg."

"On the contrary, I think you're doing great." He pushed off her coat and got rid of his. Their blended wool heaped on the floorboard, he smoothed the fleecy angora spilling around her shoulders. "Tell me what you're thinking."

"I'm thinking that I'm making a total fool of myself and I should be embarrassed, but I'm not. That I'm scared of what I'm feeling because I'm not even sure what it is—if that makes any sense."

"Makes sense to me."

"It does?" His nod, the stroke of his thumb over her cheek, had a wonderful, soothing effect. She relaxed, feeling...okay. Okay with him, with herself. How he'd done it, she didn't know, but somehow

Greg had shifted the moment into one of natural ease. "Do me a favor?" she asked.

"For you, anything."

She believed that, just as she believed he could guide them more smoothly than could her rusty confidence. "Would you take it from here?"

"Love to. But Chris, how far we take it, that's up to you. I won't stop until you tell me. It's not in me to be noble when you make me hard with just a smile."

"You're very good for my self-esteem." *Whoa!* She was flying on the wings of his earthy praise, giddy with the thrill of a woman empowered by her sexual allure. Testing it, she murmured, "I'm smiling, Greg. Are you…hard?"

He kissed her palm, then settled it over the straining of his fly. The air trapped in her throat rushed out as he slid a hand up her skirt. A single finger licked her crotch.

"Are you wet?"

"Heaven help me."

"Let's hope so, because any intervention won't be coming from me." He pressed her down on the soft vinyl and shifted them until her knees were spread and his were bent against the door. Greg tossed off her shoes. His thumb worked the arch of a stockinged foot as he said quietly, "I dreamed about you last night. It was a very erotic dream."

"Then maybe we were having the same dream." He rubbed against her, reminding her of how empty she'd felt upon waking. More, how empty and aching she was now.

"I always did wonder if women could have wet

dreams. Should I take it there's at least one woman who does?''

Chris began to wonder if a woman could orgasm in the front seat of a car without so much as a kiss.

"Kiss me," she demanded, desperate for the taste of his mouth, for more than the slow lift and press of his hips.

The sound he made was somewhere between a profanity and a blessing. Then his mouth was everywhere but on hers, laving her neck and bathing her ears between whispers of hot, urgent words. She ravaged his mouth, frantic to shut him up before she begged him to make good on his wicked suggestions. He returned her kiss with a stunning fury while his hands traveled under her sweater and slowly inched it up until he was fingering the front clasp of her bra. "Let me," he said in a low, persuasive voice. "Let me." And she did.

It was the touch of a man who knew exactly how to touch. And it was the tentative touch of memory, discovering the wonder of a female body. She was coming undone and Chris didn't have the want or the will to stop him, not even when he released the button of his jeans. She knew what was next, and then, there it was, his hand moving hers to the zipper.

"Do it," he urged her. "You want to, Chris. Do it."

She hesitated. He wedged a thigh between her legs, then pressed with a steady rhythm. "While you make up your mind, let's see if I can sway your decision."

He was good at this—too good. But she couldn't fault him. Greg was honest in his seduction. And

Chris was honest with herself. She very much wanted to be seduced.

She drew down his zipper.

"Don't stop there. Take me out. Touch me."

Being seduced was one thing; seducing him, another. As if he sensed her desperation to let go, he kissed her with a tender patience. Sometime in the midst of that kiss, he took hold of her hand and guided it to do what he wanted. *What she wanted.* She wanted to feel him; she *did* feel him, warm and sleek, virility pumping within her fist until she pressed him against the barrier of hose and panties.

"Pull them down," she said urgently. "Do it before I change my mind."

CHAPTER FIVE

HE WAS QUICK TO accommodate her, taking them down as far as he could. The small space of a front seat made it awkward, but no less exciting or agonizing as he played her so right that she gripped his wrist and led him to finger her inside. His rough groan was infinitely arousing, calling up the whimpers, mewling little gasps, that broke from her throat.

But then he was no longer stroking and neither was she. Together they held him poised, dangerously close to the point of no return. All it would take was a "Yes" and he'd plunge.

"I won't hurt you, I promise. It'll be good. I'll make it so good for you."

"No—no. Anything but. I'm not ready for this, Greg."

He nudged her with a tempting glide between the slit of her folds. "Your body says that you're plenty ready, baby."

"My body, yes. But..." She wanted to cry. She wanted to say the hell with it and just do it. She'd thought that she could, but now that she was here— No, she *wasn't* ready.

His breathing was ragged, his face etched in pained, severe lines. And his voice, it hurt a little to hear because it was terse with the effort to sound calm.

"You're telling me 'No' and I'll honor that. Your body, your choice. But to come this far and leave me hanging— Chris, I feel like I deserve an explanation."

Chris couldn't bear for him to think she had less respect for his body than he'd shown for hers. And so, painful as it was, she forced the words.

"There was a man I got involved with about a year ago. An old friend, actually, who did a lot of hand-holding before he admitted to wanting me for a lot more than a friend. I knew he cared more in that way than I did, but I was lonely and the hurt wasn't going away. I told myself that I could heal faster, come alive again, by going to bed with him. I did...but it didn't work out. I—I..." A tear slid down her cheek. Greg's eyes glittered with an incisive hunger, but the fingertip he swept over the tear was amazingly tender.

"What happened?" he asked gently.

"I did something wrong. Our clothes were off and—and I did something wrong. It was just that I loved Mark so much, I missed him so much. Time was supposed to make it better, but—I couldn't get rid of his clothes, couldn't stop waking up every morning and my first thought was 'Where's Mark, why isn't he in bed? Oh, that's right, he's dead. Dead, dead...*dead.*' How could he have done that to me? Leaving me before I could tell him that I loved him, one last time. Make love to him once, just once more. I never got to tell him goodbye. He was there and then he wasn't and if I just could have told him—but I couldn't and so I did something wrong."

"Shh, shh. It's okay, you don't have to say any more."

"But I want to, I—I need to. I've had this bottled up so long, it's been like a cancer eating me alive. That night, while another man touched me, I closed my eyes and pretended Mark was there, that it was him instead. I wanted him to be inside me and... and..."

"You said his name."

"Mark," she whispered brokenly. "I called for Mark and then—then I was alone. Lying naked on a bed and watching this man I thought was my friend fling off the sheet. Not a word. Then he was jerking on his clothes and I was talking, trying to explain, to apologize—but he was walking out. Out of his own bedroom where I couldn't get his name right, out of the house I couldn't drive away from fast enough. Out of my life. We'd gone to the same church and he even transferred his membership. I think maybe he loved me but he knew I could never love him back."

"Chris." There was a wealth of sympathy in the thumbs that stroked the wetness coursing down her cheeks. But there was more, a certain male selfishness Greg didn't try to disguise. "He shouldn't have left you like that. I'd like to say I would have behaved better, but I'm afraid I might have been worse. I don't think I could have managed the grace to stay silent."

"I wish he hadn't been. The silence was ten times more horrible than anything he could have said. I felt like I'd cheated on two men, not one, and... It was a nightmare, Greg, a nightmare."

"I'm sure it was." His simple acceptance was exactly the right amount of comfort and Chris took it.

All cried-out, she felt cleansed, freed from sickbed sheets that had been mummy cloth silencing her body, her breath.

She wanted to thank Greg but it didn't feel right. Something about him said her gratitude would take away from what he'd gladly given.

"You know, Greg, I can hardly believe it myself, but in a matter of days you've come to know me better than the people who've known me all my life."

"I like that. I like it a lot." He didn't return her smile. Indeed, he got rid of hers with a sudden and hard, tongue-thrusting kiss that left her speechless when he was done. "Know me better, Chris. Know me well enough to realize I won't be any man's stand-in, ever. Let's find out who you're really with tonight. It's something you need for yourself, and I want to be the one who sees to that need."

"Greg, I—"

"Don't say my name again. Don't say anything until you don't know where you are or what you're doing, you only know you're calling for someone to be inside you. Me, Chris. It's going to be me who takes you there. And it's going to be me you ask for when you're ready to take it all the way. I'll make sure you get the name right, trust me."

A man in his element, he made all the right moves. Kisses and more kisses, hot and deep. Hands wooing her with a perfect balance between gentle persuasion and rough demand. There, on the breasts he bared to the chill air and heated in his mouth until steamy windows shut out the pale sliver of a moon. And there—"Yes, please, there"—where he drew fluid circles and her body grasped for more than a mock coupling.

Greg…Greg…

That's it, yes…yes, that's it. Good, so good, baby. But it's been too long. Again, you need it again…. That's right, take it. Take it and say my name.

How many times she said it, she didn't know, only that it was his name she cried out, pleading for him to be inside her and why, *why*, wouldn't he be there? His hands, his mouth, his teasing thrusts, they were everywhere but inside her.

He didn't stop until she sobbed for him to quit, she couldn't take anymore. Her body listless, her head slumped to the side, she couldn't bring herself to look at him.

Perhaps he intuited her need to regain some sense of self, or maybe he was struggling for his own control. Chris was too fragmented to care about the reason, just grateful he gave her time to collect the scattered pieces of herself before he firmly turned her face to him.

What she saw was a starkly honest man. One who was pleased with himself and with the woman he had so well pleasured.

"Just a little incentive, something for you to think about." He folded her palm around his erection. "You're a sexy woman and I'm a needy man who doesn't have time to waste. Cards on the table. I want to keep things square."

"I have no false illusions, Greg. We have no future."

"Maybe not, but that doesn't mean we can't take something with us when we go our separate ways."

"I'm not sure what you're after."

He was quiet, pensive, as he stroked her hair, and then he said, "Tell me, Chris, did a man ever talk dirty to you in bed, or explain, graphically, exactly what he wanted you to do to him?"

What? Startled beyond speech, she was glad the word hadn't slipped out and given her away for what she was: a woman who'd lost her virginity to the man she'd eventually married. A wonderful man who most certainly had *not* talked dirty and still made her feel plenty satisfied in the sack. She hadn't needed any comparisons to know what they had was good.

"Why do you want to know?" she finally asked.

"The same reason I want to know if you ever told a man exactly what you wanted."

"Well, I...I never had to. I mean, he always—"

"Knew what to do?"

"Yes."

"But how could he know exactly what you wanted if you didn't tell him? Was he a mind reader, by chance?"

"No, an accountant."

"Well, that certainly explains it."

Chris wasn't sure, but she thought Mark had just been insulted. Or maybe Greg was making a joke about her evasion. Whatever his intent, he'd definitely gotten her attention.

"I wonder," he said casually, "do you like oral sex?"

"Oral—" Good Lord, where was he going with this?

"A nod or a shake will do."

Finding her voice, she blurted, "It's fine!"

"Fine. Hmm...I see." He tapped his chin and stared at her quite thoughtfully. "Do you swallow?"

"Sw-swa— Are you trying to shock me?"

"If I wanted to shock you I'd tell you exactly what I'd like to do to you. But if you want to know, you'll have to ask."

Did she swallow? At the moment she was swallowing what felt like cotton. Greg obviously had a purpose, a goal she was suddenly curious to have defined. Licking dry lips, she made herself say, "And what exactly is it that you'd like to do with me?"

His smile was thin but definitely pleased. She felt as if she'd passed some sort of test from a tough teacher who very much liked her answers.

"To be exact, I want to make love to you like you've never experienced it before. Very nice, very slow and easy—for starters."

"For starters?" she repeated.

"Surely you don't think that's where it would end."

Not sure if she wanted to know, but too curious not to ask, she did. "Where would it end, Greg?"

"I have no idea, but I'd like to find out. I'm very open to suggestions and I'm not shy about making my own requests. If you want me to be more explicit, I'd be more than happy to give you a taste of talking dirty in bed."

"*No!* I mean, no, that's not necessary. I get the picture." When he grinned, she added, "I think."

He kissed her then—a generously sweet, disturbingly demanding kiss that confused her even more.

"You're killing me, Chris, killin' me. Don't keep me hanging, I need your answer."

"You'd get it a lot sooner if I knew the question."

Something between a groan and a frustrated sigh passed his lips. "Look, I realize what kind of woman you are, and I respect you for not being cut out for an affair with no promises attached. What I want with you isn't so simple or cheap. See, I have an appetite that hasn't been fed in some time because I've become rather particular. You suit my tastes and they're…unique."

Hesitantly, she whispered, "Perverted?"

He considered that. "I don't think so, but I suppose it's a subjective opinion. I'd never want you to do something you didn't enjoy. Like I said, that's not my style, and besides, it would defeat my purpose."

"Which is?"

"To explore each other. No expectations, nothing to lose, the field wide open—between our legs and, where it gets really interesting…in the mind."

Chris tried to absorb what he was saying. An affair, unique tastes, exploration. It began to fall into place and she realized he'd left something out. *Discovery.* But discovery meant change, and change was often threatening.

"Does this mean if I want to see you again, you have some expectations, after all? That if I simply want to take in a movie and enjoy your company, it's a no-go?"

"We can go wherever you want and talk until the conversation runs dry. But it'll always come back to this." This, where he pressed himself against her and remained with a still pressure. "I want this with you too much. You deserve to know I won't play fair, that I'll press every button you've got to get what I want."

"You're warning me, that seems pretty fair."

"Not hardly. It's strategy." He shook his head with a laugh that wasn't really. "What I wouldn't give to be the kind of man you could love as much as you did your husband."

"No man, Greg, *no man* is worth loving that much again. I'll never let it happen," she vowed. "It's taken me too long to find my way out. I won't be setting myself up for another fall."

"But you'll remarry, won't you?"

"I hope so. You might like living alone, but I don't. I'm a nester and I'd like another child before my time clock runs out. The problem is finding a man who doesn't expect too much emotionally and can settle for what I can give."

"Lets me out. I could never be that man any more than the one who spoiled you for the likes of me. You'll meet someone, though. Someone willing to just 'settle.' I doubt you'll be happy, but maybe you'll be satisfied with the lucky bastard who wins the girl I let get away twice."

"Thank God I'm not in love with you." Tracing the line of his thinned lips, she was honest about the threat he posed: "You're everything I'm not looking for and I think you could still break my heart."

"Mine's already broken. You're everything a man could want and fall in love with way too easy. You're poison, baby. Pretty poison for someone like me."

It was, without doubt, the sexiest compliment she'd ever received. But from whom? The more she learned about him, it seemed, the less she knew.

"And what are you like, Greg?"

"I'm not so sure if I want you to know." His gaze

locked with hers while she waited him out. "All right, then. There's a good dose of anger, even some hurt, but I bury all that in my work. I've dished out my share of heartache and moved on while doing what it takes to climb up the ladder. I like being top dog, power's my fix. I try not to abuse it, but I have. Sometimes regretting it, but never when the means are worth the end. I know what and who I am, and make no excuses either way. I'm not a bad person but I do have some critical flaws. Now that you have more goods on me than most, will you see me tomorrow night? We both know the score."

He'd told her more than she wanted to hear. The score was: There was a lot more at stake than what she was ready to risk. Maybe Greg wouldn't break her heart, but he'd make sure she never forgot him. Once she hooked up with an altogether-decent man who made a model father, she'd have more than one ghost to deal with in and out of bed. One was dead, but as long as the other was alive, one chance meeting could pull the rug from under her firmly planted feet. No matter how much she had, that's all it would take for her to know she didn't have it all.

"I have to think about this," she finally said.

"Fair enough. You've got a phone book. Use it when you decide you're ready to move on."

CHAPTER SIX

"CALL ME." Greg kissed her cheek beneath the front-porch light. He waited until she'd passed through the unlocked door before returning to the car. There, he gave a short wave.

Chris watched until the taillights disappeared, still unsure if she would see him again.

Passing through the hallway she heard her father's snore from an open door, then low murmurs from the bedroom Rick and Tammy shared. Chris's smile held a bit of a smirk. For once, they weren't the only ones with a private agenda.

Her knees were still shaking. Wanting a man who thrilled her with a whisper of "You're poison, baby" was dangerous for a woman who'd always believed in commitment before sex. This time there would be no commitment, and she still wanted the sex. Passing her finger through a candle flame was one thing; walking into a bonfire was a good way to get burned.

Changed into her flannel pajamas, Chris sat on the edge of her old bed and stroked Audrey's hair. This was her ultimate responsibility. This child who had kept her going when she'd wanted to give up. A little girl who prayed for a daddy she didn't have.

"Maybe in a couple of years. I'll hold out for the best, when it comes to you," Chris whispered to the tight ball hugging a Barbie doll. Though Greg wasn't in the running for future dad, he'd proved a real ace when it came to a child's whimsy. Slipping the note he'd suggested under Audrey's pillow, Chris was certain a mother-daughter date for the skating rink and a bunch of quarters for video games was a super-good surprise.

The possibility of a movie and popcorn she'd left out. After all, she might still be foolish enough to dial the number she didn't need a phone book to recall.

"YOU'RE DOING IT AGAIN," Tammy observed.

"What?" Chris drummed her fingers on the breakfast-nook table while she eyed the kitchen wall phone she'd monopolized as a teen. And now, here she was, an adult visiting her parents, afraid to go near the thing lest she use it.

"*That.* Are you expecting a call?"

"Yes—no." She'd hoped for one to nudge her decision. Clearly, Greg had meant it when he'd put the ball in her court. More than in her court, the damn thing was pinging around her brain like a pinball machine stuck on automatic return. Even in her sleep she'd been betwixt erogenous replays and half-awake glimpses of Audrey's trusting face on the next pillow.

Chris looked at her watch: Six-thirty and counting. If she counted much longer they'd lose one night out of five that couldn't be recaptured. If she could just keep counting, he'd be gone and so would she. She'd pack Audrey up and head for Lubbock with morals and pride firmly intact, an untainted woman, suitable for a man looking for more than a hot fling.

No expectations, nothing to lose, the field wide open—between our legs and...

"Chris, are you feeling all right?"

"Huh? Oh, sure, I'm fine. Why?"

"Nothing, just that noise you made. Kind of a...groan?"

Between our legs and in the mind... Six thirty-three. *I'd never want you to do something you didn't enjoy.... I want to make love to you, very nice, very slow and easy....*

"You're sure the leftover ham didn't upset your stomach?"

I have an appetite that hasn't been fed in some time....

"Or maybe it's the flu. You look so flushed and— Why don't you go to bed and get some rest?"

A vision of Greg in bed didn't provoke thoughts of rest. One call and... And what if she couldn't face the mirror in the morning? She could bail out, some the wiser for her bad judgment, couldn't she? And at least she wouldn't spend the rest of her life wondering what discoveries she might have missed. *You need it. You want it.*

She was taking the risk.

"Think you could help Mom watch Audrey tonight?"

"No problem. Are you going to lie down?"

"Not here." Rising, Chris put a finger to the secretive smile framing her lips.

"Are you sure about this?" Tammy stroked her stomach like a worry stone, but the smile she returned was intrigued.

"I need some memories, Tammy." The previous

night's images continued to barrel through her brain and shoot down to her belly, pulling it tighter than a piano wire. The chord it struck rippled into a crescendo, giving a quiet passion to her voice. "I need new memories to compete with the old ones that I've let hold me back."

"Then what are you waiting for? Go for it." Tammy gave her a thumbs-up as Chris headed for the phone.

Not giving herself time to hesitate, she dialed. On the fifth ring Chris silently damned herself for assuming Greg was sitting by the phone, waiting for her call.

"Hello?" he answered, out of breath.

"It's me. I was afraid you weren't at home."

"And I was afraid I'd miss your call while I jogged off almost a day's worth of pacing the floor."

Taking heart that there was at least one man who baby-sat the phone, she said clearly, "I'm ready, Greg. Ready to move on."

An hour later she turned from his side at the car to wave. From the front door, Audrey waved back, looking curious, confused. And hopeful.

The next one's for you, daughter. But this one's for me.

CHAPTER SEVEN

"You don't waste any time, do you?"

"No time to waste." Greg's grin was cagey as he watched Chris's foot tap against the thick carpeting—high dollar, in keeping with the posh lobby, which she apparently found preferable to look at than him while they waited for the elevator.

The doors slid open but she didn't move. When her hand shot out to catch the closing metal, Greg breathed a sigh of relief. Though they were alone, Chris stared at the escalating numbers until they reached the top floor. He noticed she seemed to flounce her way beside him as they strode down the gold-sconced corridor.

"Why do I get the feeling you're a little irked?"

"Maybe because I am. I thought we'd slide into this instead of me feeling like a call girl who phoned up her john."

Greg subdued a chuckle. Enjoying himself at Chris's expense wasn't really fair, but he wasn't above making her sweat after she'd kept him sweating all day.

Wanting her to verify her decision in no uncertain terms, he tapped the electronic entry card against the door where they stood. "Sure you're ready? You can still back out."

Chris grabbed the plastic and shoved it into the slot. At the sound of a buzzer, she thrust the door open.

"Wait." He tossed a light bag through the doorway, then scooped her up. Carrying her over the threshold, he realized how fragile she felt in his arms. The purple-sweater dress she wore was designed for a leggy, thin frame that could use the illusion of an extra ten pounds. Maybe he should have fed her first. Better yet, room service; they could feed each other.

The door closed and he heard the catch of her breath in the dark. The effect it had on him wasn't to his liking, making him want to ease the apprehension he suddenly felt badly for creating.

"You think we're here so I can get a piece—no champagne, no flowers, lie on your back and spread 'em, let's do it so we can do it again before the clock strikes twelve—right?"

"Aren't we?"

Greg slid her down his length. He could feel her trembling and it touched a soft chord inside him, damn her. And damn her some more for shaking even harder as he turned her in his arms and pressed his hardness against her belly.

"If you're so nervous about being here with me, why aren't you making tracks to one of those taxis outside? It's not too late. In fact, I'll even pay your fare."

Her arms were slow to come around his waist but once there, she clung tighter than a miser to his last dime.

"It's not you, Greg—it's me. I *do* want to be here. Just give me a minute to get my bearings."

"A minute? Take an hour, take the whole night. I'm in no rush unless you are."

Her shivering stilled. "Then why are we here?"

"A piece of action, Chris, isn't simply permission and submission. That won't cut it with me. Nothing's going to happen unless you're in heat."

"What's that supposed to mean?" There was an edge of indignation in her tone and he was glad to hear the spark.

"It means you have to want me enough to light *my* fire. You're not an easy lay. These days, neither am I." Her off-the-shoulder dress gave him access to her collarbone. Lips pressed into the indentation of soft flesh, he murmured, "When you can't get my clothes off fast enough, when you can throw out every inhibition and feel good about it, *then* we can move on. The first move has to come from you."

"You're asking for a lot."

"Yeah, I am. No shutters, no limits, adults only and regrets not allowed. Those are my terms and you might as well know that I'm not one for compromise." When she stiffened slightly, he asked, "Remember what we agreed we missed most during the holidays?"

"The privacy of our own homes. Some room to breathe."

"I didn't give you a Christmas present. Consider this a belated one for us both." He flicked on the lights. Her gasp of delight made the trouble he'd gone to well worth the effort. Greg watched her lean over the entry table where two dozen roses bloomed in rainbow hues. "I never send flowers if I think they're expected. So I'll know next time you least expect them, what's your favorite color?''

''Yellow. Purple. Red. Any of them! All of them! *Flowers*.'' She sighed. ''It's been so long—thank you, Greg.''

The hint of moistness she blinked away squeezed something inside him. *Not the heart, can't be the heart.*

''Glad you like them,'' he replied gruffly. ''Go on, kick off your shoes, make yourself at home. No need to be polite or watch what you say. Wanna strut around naked? Be my guest.''

Her lilting laughter as she flung both shoes away accompanied a soft thudding sensation in the region of his solar plexus. It grew louder, harder to ignore, as he helped her out of her coat, then louder still as he hung his herringbone jacket next to her gray wool in the entry closet. Staring at the hard wooden hangers, companionably nestled side by side, he jerked them to opposite ends. Jaw clenched, he hooked an arm around her shoulder and led them to the kitchen.

''High on style, low on function. But it comes with a microwave and I happened to bring along the popcorn. Not theater fresh, but it'll do. As for the movie, if you don't like what's showing on pay-per-view, the management told me they have a load of videos to choose from.'' His kiss was short but not too sweet. Sweet was dangerous, a lowering of defenses he couldn't afford. Chris was too sweet, that was the problem; but once she cut loose and quit being such a good girl, he'd be fine. ''Still irked?''

''Are you kidding? This is great!''

''Let's check out the rest.'' In the bedroom, a big

mahogany poster bed with a lace coverlet was the centerpiece of the inviting antique decor. The bottle he'd ordered was snuggled in a silver ice bucket and positioned where he'd requested it: in the middle of the bed.

"Champagne! And look, pink flowers painted on the glass! I've never seen such a beautiful— Wait, yes I have. On "Dallas," that's it. The Ewings used to drink it at Southfork and— This is marvelous, Greg, just marvelous."

Did she have to sound so ecstatic about the very things he'd hoped would impress her even half this much? Ah, hell, he'd milk it while he could and impress her some more.

"Perrier-Jouet, 1982. France. Not their best year, but it'll do." He grabbed the bottle and offered it to her flung-out, I-don't-believe-this arms. "A tiny region in France thought up champagne and after spending some time there, I don't think much of impostors." Rolling up his sleeves, he turned his attention to a cheval mirror angled in the corner.

Covertly he watched her as she traced the hand-painted glass, green against a ruby nail—sliding it against the trickling moisture and making his testes ache for her palming, the light flick of her nails searching, moving, pressing.... Tearing his gaze from the mirror, Greg silently counted to ten, then turned to face her, still unsure if he was capable of vocalizing more than a succession of groans.

"Want me to order up some caviar and chocolate-dipped strawberries?"

"And spoil dinner? Popcorn and champagne, sounds like a feast to me." He coveted the fine arch of her neck as she threw back her head and laughed joyously. "Greg Reynolds, where have you been all my life?"

"Iraq. Russia. Thailand. Europe. You name it, I've been there. But if I could choose any place in the world, this is where I'd want to be." Fishing a coin out of his pocket, he brushed his erection and winced. "Let's try out the bed." He made a hard toss on the mattress. "Didn't bounce. But I'll forego demerits if the sheets are extra crisp and clean."

"Should we turn down the covers and find out?"

"If we did that, they wouldn't be too crisp and clean by the time we crawled away." When she bit her bottom lip, he lifted two crystal flutes from the nightstand and pinged rims. "It's your call. Flop on the bed while I spring the cork or get your butt out of here before I start talking dirty."

"Don't forget your quarter," Chris said over her shoulder as she made for the door. "You might need it later for a tip on the pillow."

The coin he left behind for good luck but he brought the glasses along. He settled them by the champagne she had placed on the mantel, above the gas logs that he turned on in the hearth. Amply realistic, the fireplace was a nice touch, set a cozy mood.

Chris stood at the picture window, surveying the vista of headlights far below.

"They look like stars on a clear, black night."

"Damn pretty sight." And he didn't mean the skyline.

"It's beautiful," she breathed. The touch of his broad palm tightening on her waist made her feel utterly feminine and deliciously warm. Pivoting, she laid her hands on his chest and leaned her forehead against his silk tie. Was she really here? Wooed with champagne and flowers by this mysterious man.

Finger to chin, he tipped up her face and kissed her softly, deeply—a kiss he spiked with a taste of demand. It left her feeling a little woozy.

"This doesn't seem real."

"Believe me," he assured her with a gentle bump, "this is as real as it gets."

His smile, that trademark naughty-nice flash of his teeth, should be illegal, she thought. It simply wasn't fair for any man to be able to turn a woman on with an easy half-twist of his lips. Staring at them, she wondered how many women had fallen victim to their lure. It bothered her to think of herself as the latest number in a long line of predecessors. And so, she tried not to think it.

"What I mean is, for our lives to go in such different directions and wind up here. It's too crazy. I keep expecting to wake up and realize I dreamed the whole thing."

"Does that mean you'd look on the next pillow and wonder why *I* wasn't in bed?"

His reference to her painful confession caused her to step back. He bridged the slight distance with a firm grip on the hand she'd laid over her heart. Pulling her to him, he stroked her arms, warming their sudden chill.

"Supposing you did," he went on. "I can only hope you'd wish I had been more than a dream."

No dream, this. Greg was a wild card and his squeeze of her buttocks was more than a reshuffling of the deck. With his soft bite to her earlobe, his murmur that the next move was hers, Chris felt she was playing fifty-two-card pickup.

"What are you in the mood for? I mean, what kind of movies do you like?" Breaking away, she hoped her lunge for the movie guide didn't look as frantic as it was. "Let's see, what shows do they have that won't hit the video stores for another month?" Flipping past the Adults Only section, she tapped an action-adventure flick. "How's this?"

"I got enough of that on the job to last me a lifetime. Did you ever see *Same Time Next Year?*"

"One of my favorites."

"Mine, too. A tad sentimental but honest and sexy." She nodded her agreement but he was staring out the window gathering wool. Chris had the feeling she was the wool. A quick embarrassment for her skittish reaction caused her to toss aside the video guide.

She touched his fist, pressed against the glass.

"Tell you what, Greg. I'll call the front desk and find out if it's available. While I take care of the movie, maybe you could make the popcorn."

The gaze he turned on her was incisive, challenging her precarious composure. He studied her awhile— long enough that Chris was torn between telling him to bring the popcorn into the bedroom and making a mad rush out the door, grabbing the flowers on her way.

"Two televisions," he finally said. "You know where they are. Decide which one you'd rather watch and I'll meet you there."

CHAPTER EIGHT

CHRIS FELT MORE in control by the time Greg met her on the couch with a bowl of Orville Redenbacher's best. When he gave her a "That's what I figured" chuckle before landing the popcorn on the cocktail table, she decided the night might be salvageable after all.

The VCR and movie delivered, she said, "Ready to roll?"

"First things first." Greg's reassuring pat on her knee relieved the last traces of tension.

His discarding of foil and wire shield seemed an omen of sorts, as did his adroit lift of thumbs to the cork. As it flew, effervescent bubbles spewed upward. Before she could grab a flute, the best champagne she'd never drunk in her life went everywhere except between their lips.

Chris put her mouth to the frothing glass. With a gurgling yelp of dismay over the waste, she pointed for him to do the same, certain she had the equivalent of ten bucks in her mouth and another twenty was headed for the floor.

"A lady shucking her manners. If that's not rich, I don't know what is." Rather than slurp up the expensive brew, he slapped his palm against the rim and shook hard. The bottle ejaculated with an enthusiasm to match their grapple as he aimed for her mouth. "Open up and let me watch you swallow."

"You open up and swallow!"

"I knew you could talk dirty if you put your mind to it." He grinned and lifted the bottle to his mouth. With a swish and a wink, he gulped. Both their faces bathed, the champagne almost gone and precious little consumed, Greg licked her cheeks, then sucked her drenched chin. Doing her part in the game of cleanup, she ran her tongue against the slope of his jaw. Each shaved whisker was a reminder of their opposite genders and just how much opposites apparently did attract.

"A glass, *monsieur?*" she offered, twirling the stem.

"Throw it." He lifted its twin and tapped their rims.

"But this is good crystal," she protested.

"So? They can bill me." Pointing to the fireplace, he tossed up his glass and caught it neatly. "Ready if you are."

Chris looked from the fine crystal to the hearth to Greg.

"Okay, bud, it's your dollar." Rearing back, she hurled with gusto. He was two seconds behind her but his flute took the lead. Her own fell apart in three sections, a puny ping to his resounding shatter.

"You throw like a girl."

"I *am* a girl."

"So I noticed." Surveying the bottle, he said, "Low tide. A swig apiece and it's empty. Want to take another shot? Put some arm into it and keep the wrist stiff."

"Give me that!" Snatching the painted glass from his grip, she decided to save the remains of her encounter with a small region of France that had invented champagne. Maybe she was too American, her tastes too unrefined, but André hadn't lost its appeal. Still, what she now held was more than the prettiest bottle she'd ever seen; it was a memory they shared, and that much was for keeps.

"I'd like to have this if you don't mind."

"Want me to order another so you can take home a pair?"

Eyeing the service-bar cabinet, Chris felt a tug she hadn't acknowledged in several years.

"I'd rather have a real drink." Deciding she felt closer to being a lady of the night than the unmerry widow, she asked for and got a double brandy, straight up. Greg poured himself a stiff Scotch and settled beside her on the couch.

Chris felt him watching her as she downed a manly portion in one draw, stopping to cough, then wince before she took another gulp.

"Just curious, but did you order that because you wanted it—or needed it?"

"Both," she confessed. "It's been a while, but there was a time when I drank a lot more than I do now."

"With friends?"

"No, alone. After Audrey was asleep and the lights were out. It kept me company in bed until I decided if I didn't clean up my act, I'd have more problems to deal with than I already did. I made myself buy a new bed and once I did that, out went the bottle."

"That must've been a bad time for you."

"Bad?" She swam her tongue through the taste of memory. "Bad was good, back then, comparatively speaking."

"Wish I'd been there."

"I'm glad you weren't."

"But you are now? Glad to be with me?"

"I am. You're good for me, Greg—in a bad sort of way."

"You make me feel like a vice."

"You are!" Chris teasingly bit his earlobe and whispered, "Want to hear about my other vices?"

"Only if they're awful."

Loose was fun; another two sips and she'd be sloppy. She swirled what was left of the brandy.

"I smoke on the sly. At first I figured it might eventually kill me, then it became a nasty habit I liked too much to give up."

"I can only hope for as much for myself."

She hooted and began to wonder if she was closer to sloppy than not. Strangely, she didn't care either way. Greg had a subtle humor, and a special knack for bringing out her own. It was, she decided, one of the sexiest things about him—next to his smile. No judgment calls from him; why the hell should she judge herself?

"If the First Methodist Church could see me now, I'll bet I could get out of playing piano for Sunday school."

"From what I know about Lubbock, you might even have a good chance of getting out of your job."

"You're right," she agreed, sobering. "Sometimes I get really tired of it—the school politics, neighbors knowing each other's business, watching what I say and do so my Snow White reputation stays intact. Trying to be the perfect mom, the perfect daughter. Well, I'm *not* perfect.''

''The things we have in common, don't they beat all. Seems you're a vice for me too, Snow White.'' There was a darkness in his gaze that had the feel of a deep, wet kiss in a public place, an urgency too strong to wait for the closing of doors.

Chris tried to look away, but couldn't. When she took a quick sip of her drink, his eyes followed the movement and remained fixed on her mouth.

''So, what other vices do you have?''

Vices…vices. She was sure she had some besides her recently acquired taste for Greg. Did reading for an hour in the tub qualify? She didn't think so. What about hating housework and having a home that showed it? Not down and dirty enough, either.

''I always pick the longest line at checkout stands. That way I can flip through the tabloids without having to hide the trashy things at home.''

His low laughter eased into an indulgent smile. ''Is there a chance that you ordered a collection of oldies-but-goldies for $7.77 from the tube when everyone with a life was already asleep?''

''I was tempted, but I didn't. They lost a sale when 'Yummy, Yummy, Yummy, I've Got Love in My Tummy' rolled up the screen. Not that I didn't like the song way back when, but hey, I've got some pride.''

''Since we're baring our souls, I have a confession of my own to make: I was weak and totally without pride.''

''No. Get outta here!''

"It's in Dad's glove compartment, along with some other tapes I didn't want to move. Again. I should pay rent for the stuff they hang on to for me."

"*You* bought 'Yummy, Yummy, Yummy, I've Got Love in My Tummy'?" She cracked up and he joined her. "Boy oh boy, have I got something on you now."

"Mutual blackmail, Chris. Never can tell when a *National Enquirer* might show up in your mailbox."

"Don't you dare! I wouldn't be able to show my face to the mailman for a week."

"Want to know what's your worst vice? Worrying too much about what other people think."

"And well I know it. That *is* my worst vice and ten times harder to kick than stealing smokes in the bathroom."

"No need to steal them here." He shoved an ashtray her way on the coffee table. "Light up whenever you get the urge. Maybe I'll even join you with the cigar my brother-in-law stuck in my pocket. I'm an uncle again, as of today."

The fact he hadn't said anything until now told her where babies fit into Greg's scheme of importance. Had Tammy just given birth, Chris knew she'd have camped out at the hospital to beg, borrow or steal any cuddles she could.

"Did you see the baby yet?"

"This morning. Cute little sucker—until it wet on me. Reminded me why I'm a lot more comfortable holding a football or a front line than babies." He studied his drink, then downed it. "Sometimes I wonder if I'd given fatherhood a second shot, if I would have done better.... Hell, couldn't do worse. But I don't ever think about it too long. I've got enough guilt to deal with as it is. A double dose of shame, I don't need." He shoved his empty glass next to hers and reached for the remote control. "Oh, by the way, I'm clean."

"Better than clean, you smell great."

"Not what I meant." He shook his head and laughed as if she'd just played straight man to a one-liner. "After ending up a daddy because Arlene's mom skipped her pills, I haven't had sex without a condom since. What with the current climate, I thought that might be a concern you weren't sure how to bring up."

"Actually, I hadn't thought about that."

"Do me a favor? Think about it the next time. I'd hate to see anything happen to you. The world, Chris, it's a better place with you around."

The warm hug he gave her played havoc with her head and had an unexpected pull on her libido. His bluntness, his comfortable familiarity with the nitty-gritty of sex, seemed healthy and yet another something she could learn from Greg. Odd, though, that he was more relaxed about sex than holding a baby.

"I'll turn off the lights," she offered, needing some distance from their close encounter of the comforting kind. But his hurt spot, his sense of failure as a father, stuck with her. Trying to escape it, she hastened her pace and snapped out a silent order. *Sleep with him, laugh with him, anything. Just don't let yourself start to care.* To care was to risk that black, terrible tunnel she would never again go near. Greg had helped her to escape, and for that she was grateful, but an emotional entanglement she had to avoid at any cost. *Es-*

pecially with Greg. Audrey aside, he was too tempting and too lethal, like cheese baiting a steel trap.

Chris stopped in her tracks as he kicked off his shoes. They landed on top of the heels she'd shucked off with a laugh. No longer laughing, she watched him prop his feet on the coffee table and stretch out. His arms on the sofa's back was a natural posture for a... "Family man," she whispered, while an image of a cheese wedge sliced through her mind.

"Did you say something?" he asked, looking away from the opening credits.

"I said that I'm glad you thought this up. A relaxed evening has a certain charm for a woman who's got a sore rear end and ate leftover french fries at the rink so they wouldn't go to waste." *Good, very good,* she told herself. *Hook it to the kid and make him bring it back to the bed where he's comfortable and this whole crazy thing belongs.*

"Then it's okay by you if we don't cancel the movie and hit the bar where we could take on Generation X? Maybe show them how to swing to Springsteen—move over, alternative rock."

Time out! Okay, here's the plan—no self-respecting stud could possibly find a woman in support hose and up to her elbows in arthritis worth the chase.

"The older I get, Greg, the slower I go."

"That's good to hear. Otherwise, I couldn't keep up."

Chris frowned. He was too easy to be with, too easy to talk to. She couldn't seem to quit telling him things—little things that were somehow more revealing than big secrets. Her affection for him was genuine and that was fine. But what she couldn't—repeat, *could not*—do was let herself think of him as more than a good time on the fly.

His fly was where she angled her gaze since she deemed it safer than his couch-potato slouch.

"Sit with me?" He patted the sofa and looked even more dangerously domestic. "I won't bite."

"I'm disappointed." Her retaliatory defense got the reaction she needed to put Greg in his proper perspective. A dark brow rose over a darker glitter in his eyes. His slouch straightened and his crossed ankles came off the table. "Wouldn't you be more comfortable with your shirt off?" she prompted, ignoring the prickling sensation on her neck.

He tapped his fingertips together, as if contemplating his answer. Suddenly, he reached for the remote control. The television silenced, only the light of the screen illuminated him as he pushed the coffee table away.

And then, he worked loose the knot of his tie. Slipping it off, he slowly, suggestively, ran its length over his palm.

"Come here." His voice was smooth but rough around the edges.

Her feet were slow to acknowledge the command. Once she stood where he had indicated, between his spread legs, her lungs shut down, her stomach rolled over, and the sound of her thrumming heart filled her ears. The only thing that seemed to be in working order was her vision, locked in on the thin silk he continued to feed through a loose fist.

What was he planning to do with it? Why did he keep staring at her that way, saying nothing, and making her imagination leap in these crazy directions? She had no idea where she was, only that it was someplace promising, erotic, frightening.

His slide of the tie around the small of her back caused her to breathe out in a rush. Using it as a pulley, he drew her forward until her knees met the couch. Thank goodness for the couch, something solid to keep her knees from hitting the floor.

He gave a quick yank and she felt herself falling, guided by his hands on her waist until she was spilled over him. Her head against the crook of his neck, she felt his fingers twisting into her hair, then pulling until he stared at her, hard. Their faces so close, her halting gasps fanned his lips. The taste of danger, thick as the scent of Scotch on his breath, his voice gritty, challenging and…amused?

"What did you think I was going to do with it?"

"I—I didn't know."

"Were you scared…even a little?"

"Yes."

"Curious?" When she jerked out a nod, he said, "Curious, that's good. What about…excited? Were you?"

She was shaking, even her lips were shaking. Forcing them to move, she answered, "I was."

"Excellent." He led her hands from his shoulders to the first button of his shirt. "Anything and everything you can possibly imagine…*I want.*"

CHAPTER NINE

IF PATIENCE WAS TRULY a virtue, she decided that Greg was either remarkably virtuous or had a keen appreciation for suspense. As for herself, Chris felt like a sixteen-year-old about to lose her virginity to a much older man. Her fingers, slow and unsteady, had an uncommon amount of difficulty in releasing the first button on his shirt.

"Good," he murmured, drawing out the word like a line he slowly reeled in while she, the slippery catch, tugged against the hook she never should have nibbled. Too late to undo her decision, she tentatively pressed her lips against his throat. He tasted no less than delicious, and the sound she heard was like a low rumble of seductive thunder spurring her on. When she reached the button above his belt, he slid her fingertip over the buckle and said, "There's more."

Willing herself to shut out all thought, she allowed the flow to take her and pulled free the strip of black. The sight of mingling leather and silk did something strange to her senses. *Anything and everything you can possibly imagine.* Chris imagined the contrasting textures sliding snakelike around her waist, her wrists. Closing her eyes, she imagined his large hands, sure and sinuous in their seesaw movement, plying the binding between her legs. She felt an immediate twinge there, tightening, lingering, as did the forbidden fantasy.

It shook her, the startling image called up from some dark place she had never roamed; it did shake her. *How could she think such a thing, worse, feel so unbearably aroused by it?* The heat in her womb gathered momentum and spread up to her breasts, to her cheeks. Even the roots of her hair seemed to pulse with a peculiar warmth. They, and the rest of her, grew even hotter as his palms embraced either side of her head where he exerted a gentle but firm pressure.

"Look at me." Reluctantly, she met the scrutiny of his gaze. "You're very flushed and I'm seeing smoke in your eyes. Leaves me to wonder if you're fantasizing about something other than getting rid of my shirt, or if you're imagining being with *someone* other than me."

"No! No, Greg, I swear I wasn't pretending to be with—"

"I believe you," he said, cutting her off as if even Mark's mention would intrude on their intimate space. "Care to tell me what I caught you at?" When her eyes darted guiltily to the floor, he made an *ahhh* sound of approval. "Have you ever—"

"Certainly not," she said quickly.

"There's always a first time and I'd very much like to be the first to introduce you to that kind of pleasure."

"That kind of pleasure?" she scoffed. "Don't you mean that sort of deviant behavior?" His low chuckle made her feel like a prude just caught ogling a naughty magazine on the pretext of shaming him for his prurient interests.

"Pick them up. Both, the belt and the tie. Go on, just do it." When she began to protest, he smiled with such open encouragement that she hesitantly lifted them from the floor. "Tell me, how do they feel?"

"The silk, it's smooth and cool. The leather, warm and sturdy. The buckle's a little heavy."

"Do you feel threatened by them?"

"No." Quick to qualify that, she added, "But I'm holding them, not you."

"So you are." He took the belt from her, folded it in half and snapped the middle. The hands she'd imagined sliding the belt between her legs returned the leather to her with a casual grace. "Should I feel threatened? After all, that's a thick belt and you could hurt me with it if I let you."

"I'd never do any such thing!"

"That's good since I'm not into pain—giving or receiving it. Big difference between that sort of thing and a bedroom game of mutual trust. Believe me, Chris, bondage isn't about abuse, it's about freedom, giving each other permission to explore a very special kind of pleasure." Lifting the belt's pointed tip, he tickled her nose with the leather.

It smelled earthy, masculine, like an extension of its wearer. Impulsively, she then sniffed his tie. The subtle absorption of his cologne provoked images of clean rain and a twist of citrus on the rim of a tall, icy glass. The scent of him mingled with a vision of silk tethers gently binding wrists and ankles to the four corners of a poster bed.

Her hands began to move with a sudden impatience

and she parted the starched white material. A wide expanse of blocked muscle was covered by a thick mat of dark gold sprinkled with silver.

"I want this off. Take it off," she demanded.

"You want it off? *You* take it off."

Hungrily, roughly, she swept her palms over the ridge of his shoulders and down his arms. Cotton joined leather and silk on the floor. She rubbed her cheek against soft hair and tough muscle, drinking in more than his cologne. It was Greg she inhaled; the unique scent of his skin, his person.

He was an intensely arousing man. Without even a hand on her, she felt as if he'd reached inside to stroke the tip of her womb.

"I want you," she said.

"Then take me." Arms spread over the length of the couch in submission, he shifted his hips downward in demand.

What she felt, Chris wasn't sure; several sensations all at once, separate but interlocked. Wanting, but afraid to want this much. Standing on a precipice of dizzying height, breath held while teetering on the edge. Wings spread, feeling the power, the thrill of charting a new course, she freed his erection and thus something in herself.

Taking him, teasingly then aggressively, she was filled with wonder. It was the wonder of discovery, finding an unexpected treasure. He had given her the means, his body a pliable shovel, to unearth a gift too marvelous to be hoarded.

She shared it generously, delighting in his delight as she bowed before the giver.

WHEN HIS HEART QUIT racing like a marathon runner and his breathing was no longer a groan after groan after groan, Greg looked down, a little amazed, at the head resting in his lap.

She looked up and their eyes met. There was a glow in her face, enhanced by a mischievous slant to her smile that he'd never seen before. Not in her; not in any woman.

For once in his life, maybe he'd chosen an intimate companion worth the keeping. When her gaze lowered to his crotch, leading his to follow, Greg was sure of it.

Laughter rolled from his belly as she lifted his softening erection by the loops of a bow.

"Poor man." She sighed, "All tied up with nowhere to go."

The sight of her swirling ruby nail stopped him in mid-laugh. And then, the touch of her finger to her tongue created a sliding sensation inside him, drizzling through his chest and pooling in his gut, which felt a sudden clutch.

"I don't swallow," she murmured.

The woman was lethal. With her dip into his leavings, the skate of her fingertip over her mouth as if it were lipstick she applied, she was lethal.

Greg caught her wrist. "Feeling your oats?"

"Umm. I think I am." Softly, she confessed, "If I'd known being a bad girl could feel so good, I would have sown some wild oats before now."

His soaring elation at being the wild oats in question coincided with a disturbing stab of possessiveness. He felt like a transient staking squatter's rights, fierce in his want of the virgin soil on which he could never lay legal claim.

Legal claim be damned. *He didn't want to share.* Not with a dead husband and not with any future prospects. It was an extremely upsetting and unfamiliar sensation, not part of the game plan he'd had in mind. It gave him a sense of lost control of himself and of the situation. Instinctively, he tried to regain what he'd lost to the woman on her knees; a woman he was beginning to fear could bring him to his.

"Unless you like the floor, I strongly suggest that you head for the bedroom." Greg had the pleasure of seeing her swallow as she rose, a bit wobbly at those knees. "Oh, and take the champagne bottle with you."

"Aren't we a little old to be playing spin the bottle?" she asked, eyeing it uncertainly.

"Absolutely."

"Then why bring it? It's almost empty."

Angling his gaze to the apex of her thighs, he said quietly, insistently, "Take it."

The wariness of her gaze, the unsteady reach of her hand, stroked his dominant nature. He wouldn't hurt Chris for the world but a small taste of danger wouldn't be bad for her, either. Besides, the danger he was tasting was no little bit, and that much he was inclined to share.

Though she gripped the bottle to her as if it were a potential weapon to ward him off, Greg admired the lack of cowardice evident in her walk. *Lethal,* without a doubt.

As he untied the bow in his lap, he found himself already regretting the moment he'd have to let her go.

A grim smile touched his lips. He had no illusions about what he had to offer. Yeah, he was a poor bargain, for sure. But that didn't keep him from considering how he might manage to get a just-fallen angel to strike a deal with the devil.

CHAPTER TEN

CHRIS CHAFED HER ARMS as she stared at the bottle
on the nightstand. What was he taking his sweet time
doing while she ate the Godiva chocolate laid on one
pillow? Deciding Greg didn't deserve his, she ate the
second while she fought the urge to shove the bottle
under the bed.

This was all so disorienting, so unfamiliar. Lights
out, under the covers, *that* was the normal thing to
do—which meant it just might upset *his* equilibrium.

Deciding the dark was an ally, she went for the
switch beside the door. Her dress was halfway over
her head when the lights came back on.

"What are you doing?"

"What does it look like? I'm taking off my clothes.
Would you please turn the lights off?"

"No." He did, however, dim them. "Ask me what
I think is the sexiest thing a man can do to a woman."

As she shoved her dress back down, her glare wavered. Shirt off, pants on but zipper not quite up and
black boxers nuzzling his navel, he was discreetly
overwhelming.

"I'm afraid to ask."

"Ask anyway." He started to bypass her but re-
traced a step and lifted her left hand. On her ring
finger, he placed a kiss, then moved on to the cheval

mirror. Picking it up without so much as a heave-ho, he brought it closer to the bed and angled the mirror until she was the central reflection.

"You're a voyeur, aren't you?"

"I like to watch, but I'd rather be a participant than a spectator." He came to stand behind her and she shivered at the feel of his palms riding down her sides, then clenching the material at her hips. Pleating it, raising the hem higher, she quelled the instinct to cover her knees. "Ask me," he said again.

"All right, what do you think is the sexiest thing a man can do to a woman?"

"*This,*" he answered, shifting the soft angora to her waist. "Undressing a woman is like unveiling a work of art. One of a kind, no two alike, in shape or tastes in underwear. Will she be a Picasso, a Rembrandt, a Warhol? Arms, lift."

If he'd told her he got off on threesomes in a vat of melted butter, she would have been less shocked. But feeling his slow peel of her dress, his nuzzle at her neck as she stood there in a French-cut bra and a lacy half-slip, she was between curious and worried about his artistic opinion of her.

"Well," she asked hesitantly, "what do you think?"

"Olga, 34C," he answered with certainty as he fingered the front clasp of her bra.

So, he was a connoisseur of women's lingerie. Certain that Greg would find her lacking in comparison to his Victoria's Secret Matisses, she caught his wrist.

"I'd really prefer the lights out." And then, with rising anxiety, she implored him with a "Please?"

"Why, are you ashamed of your body?"

She wanted to say no but that wasn't altogether true. Foregoing the bra, he hooked a thumb at the waistband of her slip and began to inch it down.

"I've had a baby, Greg."

"Um...yes, Audrey. I like her, she's a sweet kid."

"I gained a lot of weight when I was pregnant." Unable to watch, Chris shut her eyes. "I have stretch marks."

"Stretch marks," he repeated in a whisper, amazingly seductive. So was the glide of his teeth against her neck. "Where are these stretch marks...on your breasts?" At her stilted nod, he lifted her clenched fists to the bra's clasp. "Take it off? I'd like to see."

She hadn't expected his gentle coaxing; she hadn't expected her undressing to be such a painful exposure. But then, she'd done it, the bra was off while she tried not to think about the worst part to come— her lower body.

The feel of a blunt nail tracing the silver paths radiating from her areolae to the whole of her breasts sent ripples of sensory delight racing along her nerve ends.

"These actually bother you?"

"They do. I wish my body was perfect...the way it used to be."

"Not me. Maturity in a woman's body is something earned and a lot more to my liking than some teenage blonde in a string bikini. The whole package, not the wrapping, that's what moves me." The slow roll of her nipple between his fingers, as if he were contemplating, appreciating a very fine cigar, caused her to whimper his name. "Open your eyes, Chris."

She did and his own gazed back at her from the mirror. "I mean, *really* open them. Look at yourself and tell me what you see."

What she saw were two pale breasts that were firm, nipples tilted up and haloed by dark pink circles. More, she saw his open desire for them, felt it in the strain he pressed against her buttocks.

"I see…a woman who's a little thin and more than a little nervous. But she has good taste in lingerie and her breasts, they're—" Her throat was tight but as she studied herself, dark hands lifting the color of heavy cream, she whispered, "My breasts, they're pretty."

"Not pretty. Baby, they're beautiful." He slid her palms over their smooth texture, then led her to cup their weight. "Touch them. They feel even better than they look."

She couldn't believe what she was seeing, actually caressing herself in front of a mirror while he watched her and groaned. But that wasn't half as astonishing as hearing herself moan her arousal at what she felt, what she saw.

"Still want the lights out?" he asked, stroking a broad palm over her belly.

"No." Leading his hands to her slip, she told him exactly what she wanted. "I'd like you to take off the rest."

"My pleasure." His pleasure was deliciously slow and incited more visions of erotic games of trust. By the time her slip and hose were off, her spine was wet from his licking kisses and she had begun to hope he'd brought along his belt and tie. A glance at the bed assured her that he had. Their presence gave her no pause for, amazingly, she felt no threat. Just anticipation of what awaited if she dared to brave a freedom she'd only ventured in her imagination.

Panties were all she had left when he softly bit the heel of her palm and then urged it over her pubis. Curling her fingers in, she felt herself through the weightless lace.

"Feel good?" he murmured.

"Yes," she answered, almost trancelike. Yes, she must be in a trance, watching another woman who'd borrowed her body all but fondling herself in front of a mirror—for an appreciative audience of two.

"Let's make it feel even better, shall we?" Together they drew down her panties and Chris wondered at what she felt: a quiet sense of bonding that was different from any she'd experienced before. Even with Mark.

The thought slipped out before she could stop it. Strangely, she realized it wasn't Mark, but Greg who would be wronged by any sense of guilt she had for their intimate connection. Mark had no place here, and here was too special to taint with regret for the comfort she greedily took.

Fingers laced with hers, Greg roamed the slight outward arc of her belly. "What's this?" he asked, tender in his tracing of a thin silver streak.

"A stretch mark."

"And this?" He guided her nail over the flair of her left hip.

"The same."

"Do you think they're ugly?"

"Not anymore."

"Glad you realize that." His palm over her belly,

he drew her to him and ground himself against her bare behind. "You've got sexy stretch marks. Don't ever forget it. I love your body, Chris. Renoir would, too—all those soft angles and classic curves. A Renoir, that's what you are. And your taste in lingerie is, well, it's you. Elegant." He dropped a kiss, a very straightforward, unembellished kiss, on her shoulder. "For the record, I've never called a woman 'elegant' before."

She was a Renoir. She was elegant.

She was in heat.

"Make love to me." Grasping his hand, she pressed it against her groin. *"Now."*

Her gaze riveted on his reflection, she saw the pleased curve of his mouth and then, something she hadn't expected—a sly expression, as if he was the host of a surprise party for her, the unsuspecting guest of honor.

Suddenly, cool air brushed her as he fanned open her lips and stared at what he exposed to the mirror. "Look at that—mmm, what a gorgeous view. Help me out and tell me what you'd like me to do with this beautiful little joy toy of yours."

"Greg, *please.*"

"Greg, please," he echoed. "I like the sound of that. Go on, then. Please…what?"

"Touch me," she whispered. When he hesitated, she demanded, *"Touch me.* I want you to touch me." Then she added, "Please, Greg."

"Ever the lady, aren't you? I'll have to see what I can do about getting rid of some of those manners." He touched her then, a svelte glide, a single stroke. "There. Now what?"

"Damn you, Greg," she cried, panting.

"I like that even better than 'Greg, please.' Once more now, but this time with feeling."

"I don't believe this—damn you!" Swinging around, in frustration she struck her fist against his chest. He gripped her wrist and jerked her against him.

"That's it, that's exactly what *I* want from you." She yelped in outrage when his fingers bit softly into her behind, then struggled in earnest as he lifted her until she was squirming against his open fly. "Passion, Chris, that's what I want from you. *Passion.* And unless I'm terribly wrong, the kind of passion I'm after isn't something you've ever had."

As if he'd accused her of being frigid, she glared at him and snapped, "That's not true."

"Are you sure? When was the last time you looked at yourself naked in the mirror and liked what you saw? When was the last time you were so hot to have a man touch you that you told him so instead of assuming he knew that's what you wanted? And when, tell me when, have you ever hit a man because he wanted an equal partner in bed and you didn't want to accept responsibility for your needs?" No longer resistant but still flushed with the fight, she met his narrowed gaze and shivered. "Meet my need and tell me yours," he said with an ache that stunned her. Touched her. Undid her.

He began to slide her down. Chris shimmied up and locked her legs around his waist.

"Carry me to bed, just like this."

"And then?"

"Then I want you to undress for me and after that, I want you to kiss me."

He rubbed his lips over hers. "Here?"

"Yes, there."

Lifting her higher, he tongued a nipple. "And here?" Her languorous sigh proved answer enough. "Anywhere else?"

"My sexy stretch marks need you."

Her soft laughter trailed them to the bed. There, he laid her beside leather and silk, wondering if Chris would sweep them away. But no, she stroked them, allowing him to watch her shed old notions for brave new ideas. Greg considered it a priceless privilege to expand intimacy's vistas with this woman he coveted for his own. But as he slowly disrobed, he was aware of another feeling he wasn't particularly proud of: smugness born of jealousy.

Passion. Her passion belonged to him and that was something her dead husband couldn't claim. The dead husband who had taken her love with him to the grave. Greg couldn't deny that he hated the bastard a little for that. Yet his own emotions for Chris were strong enough, he believed her better off for refusing her heart to a man who'd often wondered if he was capable of that tender emotion, love.

Passion, he understood. And passion he did get.

Her body thoroughly kissed, exactly where she asked, he didn't stop until he'd reached the soles of her feet. Glorious she was in her writhing impatience, but he had a need to make it last.

Greg eyed the game pieces surrounding them on

the bed. Both players were ready, bound by rules of trust. With belt and tie in hand, he held aloft the champagne bottle.

Seemed to him they had some celebrating to do.

CHAPTER ELEVEN

"We had lotsa fun at Auntie Marge's last night."

"Uh-huh." Foot propped on a pillow in the middle of the bed, Chris painted another toenail and suppressed a moan. That toe, that very toe had been sucked less than twelve hours ago. Sucking toes, where in the world had Greg picked that up? The Middle East, Japan, maybe in France while he sipped real champagne—*who cared?*

"But the mostest fun was when Uncle Rick and old Uncle Harvey sorta had a fight playing cards. Uncle Rick said makin' up new rules was cheating and Uncle Harvey said..."

What should she wear tonight? The Olga was her best bra but the Vanity Fair was lavender and *très* risqué. Did black go with lavender? Or maybe the white tap pants.

"And then they throwed popcorn balls at each other and then they hit Aunt Tammy's bee-hind with one and then..."

Then again, she did have the whole afternoon to shop. Only, would a Renoir wear red?

"But it was lotsa fun and— Mama, what's this?"

"Maybe ivory." Finished with the last nail, Chris capped the polish and stretched.

"But ivory, that's from elephants, right? This doesn't look like it came off a elephant."

"Audrey! What are you doing with that?" Heedless of her wet toes, Chris lurched from the bed and seized the champagne bottle. "Stay out of my suitcase, young lady."

"Why're you yelling at me? I only wanted to see the pretty bottle."

Arms crossed and hiding what she held, Chris forced herself to calm down. "I wasn't yelling."

"Were too! And that's not all, you weren't listenin' to me. Ever since your friend started comin' over, it's like you're gone all the time. Why can't I come, too?"

"Because—because children aren't allowed where we go. And besides, I save all my days just for you." Dropping to her knees, Chris laid the bottle aside and, in contrition, held out her arms. "Give Mama a hug, sugar."

Audrey stepped back. "Tonight, Mama, I want you with me tonight." With a note of hope, she added, "It's okay with me if he's with us, too. We could all go to the movies and—"

"When we get back to Lubbock, I'll take you to the movies. We'll eat all the popcorn we want and—"

"But he won't be there, and I like your friend. Let him come to a movie with us. Please? Then we can be like a family goin' to the movies instead of just you and me."

"No." Her firm denial won a pout. But better a pout now than letting Audrey get her hopes up for something that just couldn't be. "Tell you what, I'll ask Aunt Tammy and Uncle Rick to take you."

Audrey emphatically shook her head. When Chris reached for her, she shot to the door and said with a sniffle, "You don't wanna be with me tonight."

"That's not true." Chris went to her and stroked the pale blond hair. "You know that's not true, Audrey. I *always* want to be with you. Tomorrow I'll make up for being gone tonight. We'll spend the whole day together, okay?"

Audrey looked away. Following her gaze, Chris saw that it was on the bottle. Deep breath. *Stop cringing, damn it.*

"He doesn't like kids, does he? I thought he was nice and he liked me, but he's not nice."

"But he *is* nice, Audrey. Greg's just not cut out to be a daddy, that's all."

"Then I don't want him to be with you. Tell him to go away, Mama. Tell him we don't like him anymore."

"I'm sorry, but Mama likes him and I—"

"Uncle Rick doesn't like him neither. I heard him say so to Aunt Tammy and—"

"Stop it!" Chris froze as she realized she had almost gripped Audrey's shoulders—to shake her. Never had she shaken Audrey, never. Only once had she even been spanked, for running in front of a car. Chris wanted to spank her now, paddle Audrey good for her childish resentment of Greg's inability to meet her expectations.

Staring at her poised hands, then the streaks resembling pale pink bracelets on her wrists, Chris shuddered. *What was happening to her?* She didn't know the woman these wrists belonged to. She didn't know this angry mother who felt violated by her child's curiosity over a bottle.

Chris shoved down the cuffs of her blouse. Gently, she cupped Audrey's cheek. "Mama's so sorry we had a fight. A few more days and we'll go home and—"

"I wanna go home now. Please, let's go home."

Chris withdrew her apologetic touch and looked away, needing to distance herself from the sight of Audrey, the shrill pitch of her demands. Waves of confusion beat at her but receded beneath the lapping vision of a white-hot night too stunning for any sane woman to regret.

Avoiding Audrey's gaze, she patted her head. "We'll go home on New Year's Day, just the way we planned."

"No!" The stamp of a small foot emphasized her shout.

"Damn it, that is enough out of you! The world does not revolve around you, Audrey Nicholson. When Mama says it's time to go home, *then* we'll go home. Do you understand me?"

"You old meanie! I'm glad you're goin' away, *glad.* I hope you stay away with your dumb old Greg, and never, ever come back!" The door slammed and Chris could hear Audrey sobbing as she ran down the hall. She heard Rick's, "Slow down, half-pint, what's wrong?"

What was wrong? *Nothing's wrong,* Chris told herself as she covered her face with her hands and struggled for as many breaths as it would take to clear her head. She had to think. *Think,* damn it. Damn it, she'd actually cursed at Audrey, lashed out at her child as she never had before. They had always been so close, and at the moment she was glad, really glad, that Audrey was gone.

God, she felt guilty for that, and for so many things. For wanting her child gone, for selfishly wanting some private something just for herself, for letting Audrey think the worst of Greg because it was easier than admitting *she* was the one who didn't want the intrusion on her sex life tonight.

Chris chafed her wrists. She wasn't herself, not at all. Maybe she *should* go home.

Her mind was in chaos, a battleground where Audrey's retreating sobs gave way to a rich dreamscape of decadence. She didn't want to be here, she wanted to be there. *There*, on her back, feeling the mattress beneath her, taking Greg's weight, reveling in being covered by his body's pressure. There she wanted to be and it was there she escaped, to a precious place of discovery, frightening and full of wonder. A place where she was anything but a mother....

LEATHER AND SILK CINCHED *in one fist, his other like a steel band gripping both her wrists. His knees strad- dling her chest, he loomed large, towering above her like some mighty warrior with the spoils of victory at his feet.*

His whisper then: "I'd never hurt you. That's why I want to know everything's all right between us here before we take this where I'm wanting to go."

"And where is that?"

"Somewhere we've never been, a place we create just for ourselves to see what we find along the way as it happens. But to get there you'll have to take the first step: I want you to give me permission to take control.''

Eyes fixed on the belt and tie, she said quietly, ''You'll be wanting to use those.''

''Absolutely. But they're merely a means to an end. What I'm asking for, Chris, is for you to trust me to treat your body with the same care you'd treat mine were our roles reversed.''

The clutch of anxiety she felt as he asked for absolute control, absolute trust, collided with a daredevil high that was more frightening than lying prone and helpless and at his mercy. How well did she know Greg, *really*? It was then she realized this was more than a game. He wanted to strip them down to the core, expose them both for who they really were beneath their civilized veneers.

Her courage faltered even as anticipation soared.

''What if I ask you to untie me? Will you?''

''Only if you say…'Roses.' *Roses*, that's the password to signal me to stop. If you say 'Stop,' I won't. You see, I want to play out a fantasy where a 'Stop' from you might be very exciting to me.''

''A fantasy? You mean, pretend something that's not real?''

''A fantasy is no longer a fantasy when it becomes reality, *ma chérie*.''

''Excuse me?''

'''*Non, non, monsieur! S'il vous plaît, non!*' would be a more apt response from a prisoner I've captured and intend to use for my own pleasure. It's a neat bit of revenge I can't resist since you're a fair *mademoiselle* born and bred by my enemy. The keep you call home is soon to be mine, just as you will be. I lust for your family's land. I lust for you."

"But why?" she asked, intrigued by the story he wove. "Why are we your enemy and why do you want to steal what's ours?"

"There's bad blood between us, *ma fille*. The land is rich and many hands tend the grape arbors your father stole from my own before you were conceived. As a boy I watched my father cut down. Only I escaped, and now, with twenty years of rage for injustice, I've returned to seize back my rightful claim. It is a day of reckoning for which you will atone, as well."

"But you said I wasn't even born and—"

"Silence! I'll have silence from you who have slept in my bed while I made my own on the grounds of strangers. You've eaten at my table and feasted when I made my meals from wild game and scraps of bread. No one to turn to, our allies were overthrown as we were. But a bitter wind blows and with it comes war. The men riding with me I've chosen for their skill with a saber, their loyalty proved from our days spent as renegades—but we are outlaws no more. We *are* the law and I am the officer in command. They follow my orders now, circling us in the woods where I rode you down.

"See the wildflowers you were gathering crushed beneath my horse's hooves, feel the warm air on your breasts, barely covered. Your clothes are in tatters. How foolish but how brave you were to struggle with me. Scratches cover my face and my blood runs hot as I force you to the ground. Look around you and see four saplings—two at your head, two at your feet. Is your heart pounding?''

''Yes...*yes*.'' The four posts took on the semblance of tree trunks and she jerked her head from side to side, staring at their ominous positions, suddenly struggling to free her wrists.

''That's it, *fight me*. You know what I mean to do and—''

''Stop!'' Grappling with him, she freed one hand and thrust at his chest. His laughter was dark and mocked her lesser strength as he easily pinned her flailing arm beneath her twisting weight and she again cried, ''Stop!''

''Stop? I don't think so. The more you fight me, the more I want you. Feel how hard I am bearing down on your hips, my mouth covering yours to taste the sweet sound of your cries for help.'' His lips were brutally sweet, stealing her breath while she felt the cinch of silk around her wrist before he led her to grip the wood. Holding it tight, holding on for dear life, she whimpered, ''No, no,'' and made a token resistance as he knotted the tie around the sapling post.

And then her other hand was pulled from beneath her. The tingle of circulation rushed through her fingers and ripples of arousing sensation shot from the soft scrape of teeth on her palm to the fierce tug low in her belly.

His nipping bites became a giving kiss pressed to where her pulse leapt in her wrist. She was riveted by the sudden snap of his belt cracking the sense-thick air, and then came the stern feel of leather looped around her wrist and fed through a buckle. It felt snug and warm as a harness while his murmured words in French mingled with the sight of him twining the belt around and around the wood.

A satisfied smile was on his lips as he taunted, "For shame, *chérie,* you've given up to the enemy much too easily. I'd hoped for a challenge but you're simply lying there while I stand over you and start to unfasten my breeches. Listen to my men cheering me on, eager for their turn at you once I'm through."

"You mean to rape me?" Fantasy and reality merged and she jerked against the restraints. "The hell you'll do such a thing! Let me go now. *Now!*"

"I'll let you go when and only when you're too weak to stand, much less walk. But as for rape…no. Rape would be too easy and I want a better victory." His thighs clamped around her legs that kicked futilely beneath him. "What spirit you have, after all. Certainly a worthy opponent to battle in bed. No, I don't believe I'll share you with my men. In fact, I've decided I don't even like them looking at you, so I order them to move on, to scout the area until I join them. And should I not appear by sunset—which is a distinct possibility—they are to make camp. You would do well to please me since it would buy your family freedom for another day."

Rising up, he clamped a palm between her legs and she bucked against his possessive grip. "I'll have this and you'll give it to me willingly."

"Never," she gasped. "Never under threat by a tyrant who wants to gloat over his conquest."

"I can see that bringing my feisty prisoner to heel is a worthy vengeance in itself. You'll vow your fealty to me once I prove what a generous master I can be. Indeed, I should think you grateful for me staking my territory and dispatching my men. Not so bad a fate, being afforded my protection.''

"Grateful? Once you're finished with me, you plan to attack my family and I'm supposed to be *grateful?*'' She stared at him, shocked to realize this was more than make-believe. He was giving her a rare access to his soldier's mentality.

"Yes, grateful. I'm powerful but I like to think of myself as fair, even when I'm taking the life of someone I don't even know. It's power that I thirst for and it's power which allows me to show mercy to those who deserve freedom. But, unfortunately, *you* don't deserve freedom or mercy at the moment. No battle is begun without the intent to win and I intend to win the ground I covet between your legs.'' Suddenly, he was off the bed and holding up a Swiss knife he'd taken from the pants he'd left folded on a boudoir chair.

The pants, the chair, they seemed strangely foreign to her, a wrinkle in the fabric of another time, a civilized age that bowed to his savage yank of the white sheet at the foot of the bed. But it wasn't a bed, it was the cushion of thick grass awaiting them, and the two carved posts framing her feet were saplings.

She heard the rending of thread as he sliced down. Three long strips he cut, then left the rest for waste.

"Your petticoat, *mademoiselle,* has met a terrible fate. Prepare to meet yours. Spread your legs.''

"I won't!'' His hands moved so fast, with such focused purpose, he simply batted away her kicks to his chest and made short work of securing first one foot and then the other to their binding stations.

Speechless at his easy mastery, she felt the rub of wood and the whip of smooth cloth that held her fast and spread her apart.

Coming to the side of where she lay, he swayed the remaining white strip between her legs, then slowly lowered the end to tease the pink tip of her exposure. Pride demanded she not give him the satisfaction of the wail trapped in her throat; but her hips felt no pride in martyrdom and thrust up, up as far as the bindings allowed.

Laughing low, he brushed the cloth over her belly, around each breast, then dangled it above her head.

"Let's see, what should I do with this?" He tapped his lips with a finger. "I suppose I could wrap it around your mouth so I won't have to listen to you scream...."

Gag her? He was actually considering gagging her? *What was the word, the password? Flowers. No, some kind of flower.* Wildly she cast about for the word that was buried somewhere and refusing to surface. And then she had it. *Roses.* "Roses" was on her tongue but in the space of a single gasp for air, his mouth was on hers. Kissing her madly, hungrily, and with a thoroughness that left her dazed, he finished with a lingering suckle of her chin.

He pinched it and shook his head.

"No, I don't believe I want this covering your mouth now that I've assured myself any screams I hear will be music to my ears. I think there's a better use for this.... Yes, perfect. But let's do this quickly because the sun is setting and I wish to see my victory in your own pleasure. Pleasure that I'm certain will be all the greater if *you* can't see." The fabric whispered over her eyes be-fore he lifted her head with a gentle pressure. She felt the tug of a knot and then the sifting of his fingers through her hair.

No sight. She heard the rasp of his breath, the absence of hers. She smelled the scent of his lust and the escalation of her own as her breast was sucked up into a haven of wet heat. Wet, dear God, she was wet, and well he let her know it with the startling upthrust of a single finger. And then she felt two, reaching so high she moaned.

"I have a taste for virgins," he whispered. "Is there a chance that a virgin you might be?"

She felt like a virgin and there was no doubt that in this place and in this moment, a virgin she was.

"I am. Please, please, be gentle with me."

"Oh, but I will. I'll fuck you ever so gently." With that vow, he withdrew his hand and she gasped at the feel of ribbed glass easing inside her. And then, then she felt the cool trickle of effervescence mingle with the stream of hot tears her body wept.

Awash in sensation, she was suddenly drowning in it, pulled under by the suckle of his mouth, the sipping sound she heard. He drank from her as if she were a golden chalice, her ecstasy a rare and heady nectar. And when he ceased his leisurely tasting, she screamed a cry of protest.

His breath on her face was flavored with the scent of woman and wine. "Could it be that my virgin captive is now a prisoner of her desire for me?" he whispered.

"Yes, whatever you say, *yes.*"

"Whatever I say, is it? I say…I want to hear you say 'Fuck me.'"

"Fuck me," she whimpered, the sound of a plea she'd never spoken before.

"How I've longed to hear those words from you. After all, some time has passed and my virgin captive is now my virgin bride. Remember with me now... how I spared you a ravishment on the ground, how I was so taken with your beauty and courage that I wanted your passion without the same resentment I harbored for the man whose name you bore. I won back my rightful claim. And I won your willing hand by my show of mercy to your kin. So merciful I am, your wish I now gladly grant."

Suddenly, the blindfold was off. She blinked against the light and saw his face bearing down on hers with an awesome intensity of raw passion. Amazingly, his initial thrust was a slow glide that stretched and filled and didn't stop until he pressed, then remained still, against her womb.

His head descended and she tasted herself on his tongue, tasted the hint of a sparkling vintage. It was a boozy sweet kiss, one she never wanted to end.

But had it not, she never would have heard his seductive whisper of, "Baby, I never knew champagne could taste so fine."

CHRIS CONTINUED TO STARE at the champagne bottle, then lifted it, kissed the rib of glass. Had it really been there where she now felt such a keen ache? And had their fantasy given way to a carnal gluttony that eased to a playful frolic, to naughty jokes and laughter? And had Greg then carried her to the sunken tub while she pretended the bottle was him and gave it a blow job to die for?

Had it really happened? It had.

So, what was wrong with Rick? Didn't he consider this man suitable for his widowed sister? And what was wrong with Audrey? Why couldn't she understand that daddies weren't the sort of lovers who made a woman beg for him in the lewdest of languages.

What was wrong with them? Rick, the protective brother with his head on straight. Audrey, the model child who had never before made such a scene as the one today and...hadn't it been said children could always spot a phony a mile away, that they gravitated to adults who genuinely liked them?

Chris dismissed the idea. Greg was no phony and Audrey wasn't used to being excluded. The problem wasn't theirs; it was hers. Her needs, so long buried, were demanding attention. She was starved for it and the man who filled those needs so frightfully, deliriously well, was feeding her greed with a voracious appetite she'd never dreamed of sharing.

Reluctantly, Chris tucked the bottle under her lavender bra and white tap pants in the suitcase. She then divided her attention between the door and the phone on the nightstand.

More than anything, she wanted to shun her responsibilities and wallow between the sheets with a man she couldn't let her child get attached to. But the right thing to do would be to find Audrey and spend the night with her alone instead of going where she already longed to be.

Chris made it as far as the door. Her hand hovered over the knob. *How many nights alone had she al-*

ready spent with Audrey? Too many. *How many more nights alone would they share?* Too many.

And how many nights did she have with Greg?

Too damn few.

Fingers curling in, her nails bit into her palm. Give in to guilt and give up a once-in-a-lifetime experience? Or spend some extra quality time with Audrey during the days to make up for the nights she desperately needed just for herself?

Making her choice, Chris put her guilt on hold, certain she'd have to deal with it later, and picked up the receiver. The wait for his voice was an eternity.

"Can you be here an hour early?" she asked. Two hours early was better for Greg. Before she could tell him to step on the gas even as they spoke, Chris hung up.

Going to the vanity, she flicked aside the blue-and-gold tassels of a pom-pom and faced herself in the mirror.

It didn't crack. She didn't look away.

"Black," she said aloud to her reflection. "Black bra, panties and hose. They match, even if you and Greg don't."

Turning from the mirror, Chris decided that she'd never looked better in her life.

CHAPTER TWELVE

HE COULDN'T PUSH IN. Even after an hour of foreplay, he couldn't push past whatever barriers her frantic hip jerks said weren't there.

Rolling off, Greg looked at the ceiling while Chris stroked his chest and asked, "What's wrong?"

"You tell me."

She gripped his erection and pumped several times. When he didn't respond, she let go and assumed his own back-to-the-mattress posture.

Their silence stretched out and she fumbled for her purse beside the bed. They'd gone there directly—the same bed as the night before, but not the same bed at all.

He reached over to his nightstand and found a match. Lighting her cigarette seemed the most intimate act of the evening.

"There's nothing wrong," she finally said, studying the smoke she sent into the tension-thick air.

"You're full of it, Chris." He plucked the cigarette from her lips, took a puff, then gave it back. "You were tight the first time, but ten vestal virgins combined couldn't be tougher to work past than this," he said with a terseness born of frustration.

He'd been so damn hungry to kiss her that he'd pulled off the road twice before they'd made it to the hotel. Even as he'd tumbled her to the bed, he'd tried to dismiss her emotional distance with every bedroom trick he knew and some he invented as he went along. Nothing.

She turned to him, head propped on her palm. And then she said, "Audrey."

"What about Audrey?"

"She neutered me, as you apparently noticed."

"I take it she doesn't approve of me."

"If she did, I'd be worried."

He managed not to flinch. Could a man feel like a hooker? Maybe so. *He* did.

"But it's not you," Chris hurriedly explained, while what had gone soft was now limp. "It's us."

"But after last night I thought— Ah, hell, I don't know what I thought. Just that it was great and we were good together."

"Better than good, Greg. Last night was incredible. It was all I could think about today until… Audrey, this afternoon, she picked up the champagne bottle."

"Nothing left to drink, I finished it off."

"You practically finished me off, doing it!" Relaxing, she laughed. He couldn't laugh with her, but he relaxed some, too, and traced her lips. Her nip of his fingertip was the second most intimate act of the night. "The problem is, Audrey wants a daddy and it's up to me to find her one."

"And a daddy I'm not, right?"

"Of course not!" Forget being a prostitute; he felt like he'd been emasculated. "C'mon, Greg, we both know what this is."

He'd thought he did, but somewhere along the line they'd bypassed the merely titillating and shared what felt like substance. It had nagged at him all day like a sore tooth he couldn't quit tonguing: What had happened? When had it happened? And did whatever the hell had happened cut both ways?

"Just curious, but what exactly do you think this is?"

"What we agreed on to begin with. 'No expectations, nothing to lose. No limits, adults only, and regrets not allowed.' A few more nights, that's all we've got, all we can ever have. After that, I go home and pick up where I left off."

But things have changed, he wanted to say. A few measly nights weren't enough to play this to its end and Same Time Next Year was too long to wait. Chris could meet someone else and there he'd be in D.C. without a chance to compete.

Sounding as casual as he could, he asked, "How would you feel about me coming to visit, or flying up to see me?"

She paled before crushing out her cigarette and immediately going for another. "I don't think seeing each other after we say our goodbyes would be a good idea."

"Why not?" he pressed, his guts knotting.

"I don't want to talk about this." She reached for the bedside light. He gripped her wrist and rolled her back. He leaned over until he was in her face. No longer pale, her cheeks were bright spots of pink.

"Know what, Chris? Every time you don't want to confront something, you go for the lights. I want them on while you answer me."

They were locked in a staring contest. Finally, she broke it. He wanted to grip her jaw and snap her around but instead, he caught her chin and fondly turned.

"All right," she said, sighing. "First of all, I have an example to set, a reputation to maintain. If we see each other, we'll sleep together—or make that, not sleep—and I can't risk getting caught."

"We could be discreet." Even as he said it, the suggestion turned his stomach. Sneaking around meant there was something to hide. No, he didn't think it cut both ways with them, after all. He could just see Chris making excuses, trying to explain him to her friends. And him? If he had her on his turf, he'd flash her on his arm like a Rolex. Hell, make her a movie marquee: *Now Showing...Man Goes from Rags to Riches and Ain't She a Million-Dollar Doll?*

"Even being discreet, Greg, it wouldn't work. As long as you're in my life I won't be able to, as you say, move on. How could I possibly go in search of The Great American Daddy if your shoes are under my bed?"

Suddenly, he wanted the lights off. Greg bummed a cigarette and lit up.

"Are you looking for someone like—" He couldn't bring himself to say the name and "dead husband" seemed a little cruel, though a little cruel he felt. Something told him that cruelty wasn't a qual-ification for The Great American Daddy. "Are you looking for a duplicate to replace the first father?"

"There could never be anyone like Mark. And even if there was, I wouldn't want him. He'd deserve to be well loved and that's something I'm not willing to give."

"But don't you think you're cheating yourself of

something that could be good by keeping that kind of distance?''

"Maybe. But it's more important to me to survive. You lost two wives. Not to death, but divorce is the next closest thing. Surely you went through some grief—''

"No grief here, just regret for bad judgment.''

"Then surely you've loved *someone* enough and lost them to understand what that does to a person.''

"Not yet. But...I guess it could happen.''

"For your sake, I hope it never does. Wanting to touch someone, to ask how their day was and really care about their answer, but knowing the closest you'll ever get is a memory—''

"So, once I'm a memory to stash away with your others—not together of course, mine in the closet, the others on their exalted altar—just what kind of a guy will you be on the prowl for?''

Direct hit, he noted with satisfaction. There was a shocked quality to her quick intake of breath, the rapid blink of her eyes as if she couldn't believe he would be so mean, that he would deliberately hurt her with his words.

"If you must know, there's a man at church who happens to be the assistant principal where I teach. We're chaperons for a school dance coming up and he's let me know that he'd like to make it a date. I think I should pursue it.''

"I'm impressed. Go on.''

"He's a widower with two teenage daughters. They sing in the choir and make straight A's.''

"They sound even more interesting than him.'' A heartbeat passed and she didn't fling his own less-than-successful attempts at fatherhood at him. *Why* was he doing this? Unless he backed off, he could forget about the few nights they had left. "Sorry, guess I'm jealous. They seem like the perfect family and that gives you a lot in common."

"He's president of the PTA." As if she wanted her lover's approval of the potential husband, she rushed ahead. "And he's very good with children. The worst discipline cases at school get handed over to him."

Yeah, great, but how does he screw? Husbands, of course, didn't *screw* their wives. At least, junior-high assistant principals who chaperoned dances and shared a hymnal with straight-A daughters—shit, that's right, they sang in the choir—didn't screw. God, he hoped not. They did, however, make love— at least often enough to have kids—and Chris had said she wanted at least one more. Not his, surely; but The Great American Daddy had the plumbing to get the job done.

Greg shut his eyes against the image of Chris going through the motions of conception. She wouldn't love the man, be it this one or another, but there would be affection, mutual respect and the standard trimmings for a commitment. To make her loveless bed and lie in it, she'd need that much.

That much was more than he wanted her to have. Selfish, uh-huh. Went right nice with a mean streak. He was some stiff competition, yessir.

Stiff he was not at the moment. But he wanted to be. He wanted a raging hard-on to drive Mr. Goody Two-Shoes out of the running, make her so sore she'd still be hobbling at the stupid dance—chaperoning with her precious reputation intact.

"He sounds like a super guy for you, Chris. Say, if he's so good with discipline cases, maybe he wouldn't mind taking a crack at Arlene." *And while she's making him itch for a new job, what say the two of us slip into the nearest broom closet and get it on until the janitor turns us over for next in line after Arlene?* Strategy. There was an angle.

"From what you've told me about Arlene, I don't think even Jerry could handle her."

Jerry. So, the jerk had a name. Easier to like him without a name, but either way, Greg didn't like him one damn bit.

"I'm sure he'd try his best, given his track record. As for mine, it speaks for itself."

"Hey, don't be so hard on yourself." After lifting the cigarette that had burned down to the butt from his lips, she brushed the ashes off his chest and kissed him where his heart thudded dully. "If it makes you feel better, you make me wish I wasn't a mama when we're together."

"You mean if you weren't, you'd want to meet me in the locker room after the first half's over?"

"I'd want to keep you there until the clock went into overtime. Heck, even when I think about you, I feel like a teenager with more hormones than good sense."

"I'll take that as a compliment." Lord knew, he could use one from her hallowed halls of motherhood. "So what about tomorrow night? Kid or no kid, I want to see you. I'll cancel our reservations and the three of us can arm-wrestle each other for the last greasy french fry, if that's what you want."

"No," she said abruptly. What had been limp was

now closer to shriveled. "Don't get me wrong. Audrey thinks you're nice—she told me so."

"Then what's the problem?"

"She's upset because I'm neglecting her to see to myself. I need you, Greg, but the way I need you doesn't have room for Audrey. Bringing you on the scene would only confuse her when the two of us are temporary. I wish things were different, believe me I do, but I'm not the only person I have to think about."

What about me? He clamped his jaw before he could ask. Surveying the surroundings, the answer was all too clear. This was it. Still, he had to push.

"Audrey seemed to like me." Weak defense but it was the best one he had.

"She did." Chris's nuzzle to his chest only made him feel worse. "And I think you're a wonderful man."

"But you don't want me to spend time with your child."

Groaning, she flopped on her back. "Damn it, Greg, I don't need this coming at me from both ends! I feel like hell after Audrey gave me what-for today and wanted to go home. Much more of you putting the screws to me and home's where I just might go."

He hadn't lost her yet and yet he was losing her already. Was it her, or was it him? Emotional introspection wasn't his strong suit but he saw far enough: Chris could love deeply, too deeply, so she refused to even give him a chance. He'd never been able to love deeply enough, a control freak who liked to get his way and usually did. She wasn't giving him his way and he was sulking. No wonder his marriages hadn't worked out. No wonder Chris wouldn't have him.

But he'd have it from her as to why not—in his face and straight from her mouth. Maybe they should end it here.

"It's clear, perfectly clear, that I don't fit into the big picture. But even in the short term, I've got some pride. You're ashamed of me and I've got a problem with that."

"Ashamed of you?" Her eyes had never looked so brown, so deep. So affronted. "Where did you ever get that idea? If I'm ashamed of anyone it's me. You're honest, I'm not. I've lied to my daughter, my family, I've lied to myself. I've lied to everyone but you—and only because you won't let me. You've been a real friend to me, Greg, and I'm already dreading goodbye. All the more reason that after we're over, we *have* to be over. Not because I'm ashamed of you—that's ridiculous—but because I could care for you too much. And that's the one thing I can't afford."

"Does this mean..." *Deep breath, just say it.* "Does it mean you could fall in love with me if you let yourself?"

She took a while to answer. "I don't know. But it really doesn't matter because I can't, I *won't*, ever let that happen. It's all or nothing with you, and falling for someone who makes those kinds of demands is the most self-destructive move I could make. Audrey aside, there might be a chance I could fall in love with you, and that's the biggest reason I won't be seeing you again once we finish what time we've got left."

She could love him. If only he hadn't been such a loser as a parent, a husband. If only she knew how deeply, how often he wished he could rise above past failure and prove himself as a father and a man. *Let it go. You ain't no daddy but your libido's working again.* Chris's confession had aroused him more than a fevered touch. She could love him—what a rush. Addictive stuff; he was already hooked.

The realization hit him with the impact of a brass-knuckled fist and all he could think was, *Ah shit, man, are you in trouble. Give her some room and get some for yourself.*

"Look, if you need to spend time with your daughter tomorrow night, I can make myself scarce. I don't like it but I understand. Whichever way you want to work it, we will."

Chris did a finger-drum on his chest. "Jelly beans."

"Say again?"

"Audrey has a weakness for jelly beans. I have a weakness for you. One pound of the suckers—bubblegum, her favorite flavor—and maybe we can reach a compromise."

"And if you can't?"

"Don't cancel the reservations anyway. Only, don't you think we should move to another room? This suite must cost a mint and we're spending all our time in bed anyway."

"You're watching my checkbook?" Greg laughed around a groan. How many women would push for a Motel 6 when they had the Ritz? None that he'd ever met. Served him right, for Chris to end up screwing with his head. Had to get it on straight before he lost his heart to a woman who took no prisoners. "It's this joint or a fast flight to Lubbock. I'd like to check out this Jerry So-and-so and warn him that he'll have me to deal with if he's not good to you. Take a second and choose."

"I choose...you." She kissed him soundly. "You have smoker's breath."

"So do you. Want to share a toothbrush?"

"And give you girl germs? I wouldn't dream of it."

"I like your germs. Admit it, Chris, a champagne bottle's safer for you than getting toothbrush cozy with me."

"Like I said, you won't let me lie. As for whichever way I want to work it, tell me, *exactly,* how you'd like me to."

As she felt for him beneath the covers, Greg stared at the ceiling. Options...strategy.... He could make sure she thought of him tomorrow with every step she took. He could make her salve his bruised ego and pump hers up so much she'd realize she had too much going to settle for a wing-tipped bore. He could make her think. He could make her pay.

If he did it right, he could possibly manage all four.

"Get dressed if you want to come with me. If you don't, I'll be glad to order up a bottle of champagne to keep you company while I'm gone."

CHAPTER THIRTEEN

STUFFING HIMSELF INTO his pants, he watched Chris shimmy into her bra, then reach for the panty hose— *ug-ly,* whoever thought those up deserved to be shot. Greg slipped into his favorite pair of loafers— *Forget the socks.* She pinched her own feet into the high heels and raced him to the door.

There, he zipped her dress—damn, but he could get used to this easy—while she adjusted the shoe that fit no better than Cinderella's glass slipper had on the bitchy stepsisters.

Chris wasn't a bitch but he'd be tempted to give up his considerable nest egg if she could see her way to becoming a bitch first-class. Then they could split, no problem.

"Where are we going?" she asked, panting.

"Shopping." He punched the Down arrow, then pinched her butt. Glancing around, she made sure no one had seen.

"Go shopping for what? It's nine o'clock."

"So?" The elevator was empty. As the doors slid shut, he pressed her against the leather-cushioned wall. Palms on her hips, he shoved his own against her and rubbed.

"What do you think you're doing? Someone could—"

"Don't worry." Hitting the Stop button between floors, he pushed up her skirt and insinuated a hand beneath her ugly panty hose. Fingering her, he said roughly, "You're wet. First time tonight. Maybe I should rent out the elevator."

"I thought we were going shopping." She clutched at his hand, but he waylaid her efforts with a persuasive entry that left her poised on tiptoe.

"What are you hungry for? I might not be The Great American Daddy, but I am one helluva cook and since you're so concerned about me wasting my hard-earned bucks, far be it from me to let the kitchen go to waste. How about leg of lamb with mint jelly— back up. No time to marinate. A tray of canapés? Perfect. They look tempting, taste delicious, and whet a person's appetite for more."

"Hamburgers," she gasped. "Hamburgers are fine. Sonic burgers are my favorite."

"Quit worrying about my financial status, would you?" Pretending to remove his hand, she gripped his wrist and squirmed down. His laugh was low and immensely satisfied. "I'm plenty solvent even if you have to be so stingy that you can't afford me. What about smoked salmon with white sauce and a few capers for garnish? Should be just your speed."

He released the Stop button.

Her hand slammed down. One on the button, the other shoved his retreating fingers back under her panties.

"Finish it," she begged with such demand that Greg decided he could be generous.

"I'm crazy about you, Chris. Every time I think of you, I want you. When we're together, I can't hold you tight enough or get in you deep enough. Crazy, you're making me crazy and I want you just as crazy for me. Only for me."

Okay, Jerry, match that. And if by some miracle you can, let's see you top this. Thumb to cleft, fingers spread against inner walls and moving, he knew how to make them weep.

Mouth open, her breath a shuddering, silent cry, she climaxed with an intensity he felt in his fingertips and elsewhere—in a place he couldn't locate but still it was there, warming him, touching him, making him feel more vulnerable and more a man than he'd ever felt before.

This part of her belonged to him and him alone and not even The Great American Daddy could take it away. Greg's smile was grim. Maybe he couldn't stop her from throwing in her lifetime lot with another man, but he could still come between them if she called for "Greg" at the best possible wrong moment. His desperation for that hold over her, his need to intimately triumph over a dead man, was a little sad, pitiful to him. That he had come to this did not make him feel proud. It was wrong, and he knew it; but he was hurting in a place she'd created, an empty spot she was refusing to fill.

The elevator phone rang.

"Should I answer?" he asked quietly as Chris put herself back together and moved to the far end. Hands gripping the shiny brass bars, she seemed to shrink into the corner. Even from his position by the doors, he could see her shaking.

"I don't care. Just hit floor number three so we

don't have to face anyone who's making that call from the lobby.''

At the third floor several people stepped on. When she made to get off, Greg caught her arm.

"Wrong floor," he said loudly enough for everyone to hear, then whispered, "Hang loose, okay?"

Chris worried her ringless ring finger. She reminded him of himself as a kid, stealing a candy bar at the five-and-dime, then being marched by his mother to the manager's office where he was sure a policeman with handcuffs was waiting. A confession and an apology had won his freedom, but he'd taken a good lesson home to remember.

If he could do the same with Chris, he might have a prayer for an extension of time.

A "ding" and an illuminated L marked their arrival.

"Let's go." Greg gave her a gentle shove and she reluctantly went. From the side, he could see her eyes darting around for a watchful guard, her feet slow but ready to run at the first accusing finger. "No one knows who we are." He felt her arm tense under his grip.

"I feel like it's written all over my face." She looked at the floor and he subdued the urge to give her a shake. "What we did was insane. What if we'd gotten caught?"

"But we didn't. The desk's over there if you want to turn us in and clear your conscience."

Her glance at him was sharp. "I can't believe you're so calm, like this doesn't even bother you. It doesn't, does it?"

"Bother me? Hell, no." He wanted her to admit

what she'd so obviously enjoyed; her shame over it maddened him, dug and bit at that empty spot of his. "I loved every gasp out of your mouth, every wet grip of my fingers, every—"

"Stop it," she snapped.

"Last I remember, it was your hand on the Stop button."

"That's right, rub it in."

"Once we get back to our room, I'll do more than that."

"Don't be so sure, you cocky bastard."

He stopped her near the exit, palms firm on her shoulders. When she tried to break away, Greg held fast.

"Unless you want to make a scene and bring the concierge over here, settle down."

"Why? So you can feel me up while he watches?"

Hmm. Chris wasn't a bitch as far as bitches went, but there was enough bitchiness there for a yelling match to clear the air. Hell, she might even have it in her to throw a thing or two. Fine line between love and hate; one could trip into the other. If he couldn't have her love, he'd take hate over indifference any day.

Greg took heart since there was nothing indifferent about the grinding of her teeth.

"You're right, Chris, I am a cocky bastard. Cocky enough to hold out on you until you ask for it. Even then, I'll hold out until you get mad and demand I give you what you want."

"The last thing I want right now is your smug attitude."

"Talk about attitude, you're pissed. And why? Because I don't play clean but you still want me. And that scares you.''

"Damn right, I'm scared. I'm scared of what I do when I'm with you.'' Waiting for a couple to pass them, she shivered, then whispered, "Last night it was bondage—''

"But you wanted it, babe,'' he reminded her.

"Greg, please, listen to me,'' she said urgently. "I was as much to blame for what happened in the elevator as you—''

"Blame implies guilt for some harm done. No one was there but us, so it comes down to you and me, and I'm fine. Did I hurt you somehow? Is there blame to be had that I don't know about? Tell me, because I'm confused.''

"*I'm* confused. Maybe blame was the wrong word, but I do know that we're pushing the envelope a little more each time and what seemed right when it happened leaves me in a cold sweat once I step back and ask myself, 'Good God, what have I done? This isn't me.' But it *was* me, and I'm having trouble dealing with that.''

"Then let me help you deal with it and tell you where the trouble really is. It's in your secret garden, the one you neatly tend after dark with me. If you hadn't noticed, I like the light. Because it's the light, Chris, that makes your garden grow.'' He softly knuckled her jaw. "Think about it.''

He released her and walked on. Hard as it was, he left her behind to retreat to the room; a room that would be empty when he returned if she hailed a cab instead.

Needing the crisp night air to clear his head, Greg waved away a valet's offer to deliver the car.

Only willpower kept his feet from racing in reverse, and that almost made him hope she'd be gone. Chris was scared? *He* was scared, more scared than the time he'd pissed his pants when a covert operation had him in a foxhole, hearing a kid on his first mission crying for Mama while four of his other men lay mangled all over his feet.

He got out with the boy. Shell-shocked, the kid ended up playing tiddledywinks in a nut ward. As for himself, he wrote to the families of the deceased, then did his damnedest to purge it all away in two weeks of R-and-R hell-raising. Eat, drink and be merry, for tomorrow ye may die.

He'd had a better chance to survive than most, sensitive situations being his specialty. But none so sensitive as this. Yeah, Chris had him scared. Even more scared than dying.

As he rounded the car, the strike of his fist on the hood coincided with the rapid click-click of high heels that went off like a machine gun in his head.

It took everything he had and then some to slide into the driver's seat without a glance in her direction. Greg gave her long enough to get in before he cranked the engine.

Breathless, she took off the shoes she never should have tried on, much less bought.

Seemed those shoes and he had a lot in common: giving Chris hell while she broke them in against the laws of nature.

The silence was taut as he drove, his pride demanding she be the one to reach out first. So far, he'd been doing all the reaching. Her turn. It was her turn, damn it, and until she took it, he was doing what he'd been trained to do so well: show no emotion while he picked up the remains of unbeating hearts and their shattered dreams of a future.

If he could do it for a few good men, he could do it for himself.

CHAPTER FOURTEEN

CHRIS STARED out the window, the passing street-lights with Christmas decorations on their posts a blur. All she could see was Greg in bed, in the elevator, in the lobby where she'd sensed his anger was really hurt.

Terrified, she was terrified to touch it. Still, she did touch him, his hand tight on the steering wheel.

"I'm sorry," she ventured.

"For what?" Voice curt, eyes straight ahead.

Actually, she wasn't sure what she was apologizing for, just that he'd seemed to expect one and she felt badly for calling him a cocky bastard. Only he'd deserved it; had even agreed and taunted her with her weakness for him in bed.

"I'm sorry that we had words. Our time together is so short, I don't want to spend it arguing."

His profile could have been carved from marble. He wanted more than an apology, she realized. Why she should be surprised, she didn't know. He *always* wanted more. For every inch she gave he wanted a dozen, and she wasn't up for the distance. Why couldn't he understand that? Him, of all people, who'd twice proved that he was no long-distance runner himself. Did he think she could break his no-win marital streak? Surely not.

Even the thought of marriage to Greg was absurd. As absurd as the Kissin' Don't Last, Cookin' Do sampler she'd embroidered for her kitchen warmed up to his spare, spotless style.

Chris wrinkled her nose with a slob's snobbish distaste for immaculate addicts. Everything in order, their obsession for just-so neatness, as if their lives would fall apart if a dish was put in the wrong cabinet—*pu—leez*. Greg was one of *those,* and what made it worse was him being a man, for Chrissakes. Last night, after he'd stripped for her, he'd folded his clothes and eyed hers on the floor. And before they'd left, he'd cleaned up the glasses they'd thrown, then checked for stray popcorn kernels. But it was his making up the bed and tightening the coverlet when the coin didn't bounce that pronounced him a neat freak of the highest order.

Funny, it hadn't bothered her last night. Then again, his demands had been of a different nature. Ever since he'd picked her up, he'd kissed with too much feeling, touched her with an emotional hunger that was all the more piercing because it was tentative, as if he was new to touching that way and wasn't quite sure how. As for his jealousy, his pressure to expand their relationship, her head was still spinning and her heart was still pounding.

Marriage to Greg? Banish the thought. He would want to possess her, consume her, and the more he pushed, the further she'd retreat. Just like tonight. And just like tonight, he'd punish her for denying him what he wanted.

Punish her; yes, that's what he'd done. He'd punished her by pleasuring her and making her admit to the dark side of her sensual nature. He was punishing her now. With his straight-ahead stare at the road, his heavy silence, he was bullying her into a confrontation.

And then, she realized. Greg wanted a fight. He was setting her up to take him on.

Chris's lips twitched with amusement as she plotted her revenge. Besting Greg at his own game was too tempting to resist. And besides, this way they could both win.

"I... Greg, I thought about what you said, about my secret garden and wanting to tend it in the dark. I decided you were right. That's why I came after you."

When he glanced at her, she removed her conciliatory touch from his ungiving hold on the wheel. He quickly recaptured her hand and brought it to his thigh.

Voice soft, with just the right hint of innocent seduction, she explained, "This garden of mine was awfully barren until you came along and gave me a taste of forbidden fruit. It scares me because...well, I do run the risk of getting snake bite. You know how snakes like gardens." She felt his thigh flex against her smooth upward brush, and then his immediate thickening beneath her cupping palm.

"I have a garden at home, Greg, a small vegetable patch, and a snake slithered out while I was hoeing one day last spring. I chopped its head off and then its tail when it kept on wiggling." The flinch in his groin did not go unnoticed.

"Anyway, after you left me, I thought about how much gardens need both night and day to grow. And how it's the same but appears so different in the dark when I can't tell what's what without a light. I'm a little night blind, so I eat a lot of carrots. I decided you're like a carrot for me.''

"A carrot, huh?" His slight chuckle told her she had gained the advantage. "A fat one, I hope."

"Long and fat, definitely a major-league carrot," she assured him. "It's a real joy to me, Greg, seeing all those colors and shapes leave my garden in a big wicker basket that's headed for my kitchen. So, there you have it, the reason I ran to you, instead of away."

"A basket of vegetables is why you're here?"

"Why, sure. I knew if I left, I'd keep seeing you as all those veggies in the basket and kick myself because—" she clicked her tongue "—oh, gee, I could have had a V-8! And there I'd be rummaging in the pantry for some junk food I didn't even want." She leaned down and kissed the straining of his fly. "I want you, Greg. You *are* my secret garden. Let's harvest everything we can, while we can. Please."

She looked up to beseech him and saw everything he didn't say. The frustration, the distress of a man who was not a graceful loser. Maybe he didn't want her to see, or maybe he simply decided to take what he could while he could, but his palm gently stroked her head as he pressed it down.

"We'll be there soon, but it won't take much." His voice had an odd sound, like sandpaper brushing velvet.

He covered her head with a portion of his coat. It took a minute perhaps, before he came. The muffled groans she heard were quickly followed by the sound of tissues pulled from a box on the dashboard and nudged toward her mouth.

Chris pushed off the coat and sat up, heedless of any oncoming traffic. Greg, backhanding sweat from his brow, appeared confused as she shook her head at his offering.

Sure he was watching, she swallowed.

"HEY, GUESS WHAT!"

"What?" Greg called back from the kitchenette as he tossed a cherry tomato into the air and caught it in his mouth. A snap of his teeth and down his throat it went. If only Chris's defenses were so easily downed.... Had to be a way; he just hadn't figured it out yet.

"There's a Harvard prof who swears Earth women have given birth to alien babies and an intergalactic race is only a generation away. Neat, huh?"

Laughing, Greg put the finishing touches on the platter and, balancing it on fingertips raised high, strolled into the living area. There he paused, absorbing the pure pleasure of seeing her sprawled on the couch, wearing his shirt and nothing but, a heap of trashy tabloids scattered on the floor.

Grinning, Chris looked up from the one she was reading. Their gazes caught and held. Her expression sobered.

"Why are you looking at me that way?"

"I like what I see." He placed the tray on the coffee table, wondering as he did what sort of home Chris had. Probably a quaint bungalow with pine floors and vintage furniture, some worn white wicker rounding out the spaces as soft and warm and invitingly messy as herself. And a porch swing. Yeah, she'd have a porch swing. One that needed painting and creaked. But she'd like it that way—lived-in.

"So, come nice weather, do you drink lemonade and sing to Audrey while you swing on your front porch?"

"How did you know I do that?"

Greg shrugged. "I just do. The same way I know you sit out there alone in the dark and listen to the crickets while you try not to think too hard but end up doing it anyway."

With a look akin to amazement, she said, "Are you sure you haven't been spying on me?"

"Not yet. Scoot over and make room for—" *Daddy.* One of his favorite shows as a kid, but Danny Thomas he wasn't. Or at least, he hadn't been. Chris made him want more than ever that second chance to be the kind of father who'd swing on a porch while he read a fairy tale to his kid.

Jeez, talk about fairy tales. The odds of that happening were on a par with spinning gold out of straw.

It felt like straw clogged his throat, a whole roomful of it, and he coughed dryly as he pulled Chris onto his lap.

"Are you okay?" she asked, putting a cool palm to his forehead. "You feel a little warm."

Toast was more like it. With her concerned little gesture, Chris was making him crash and burn, here and now. He was falling in love with her, he realized, wishing fiercely for some way to break the fall. Worse than bad, he could see the writing on the wall.

He was going down like never before.

But the hell if he'd suffer alone. Jaw clenching,

Greg swore to himself that Chris was going down with him. Be it fellow survivors or casualties, they'd share the same fate.

Grip stern on her wrist, he bit into the heel of her palm—a soft, teething gnaw that won a sigh, and then a sharp gasp when he clamped hard on flesh and muscle.

Tracing the imprint of his teeth, he said quietly, "Good thing I can't eat you alive since there wouldn't be anything left. Even for me. And it sure wouldn't be fair to Audrey, much as she needs you, along with that daddy you're hoping to find for her. Problem is, Chris, she needs more than two parents who wrap their lives up in a child because they don't have much else holding them together."

Chris glanced away. "Since when were you an expert on what kids need from their parents?"

"Since I screwed up with Arlene and got the distance to realize where I went wrong. And looking back on my childhood, I can see where my own folks made some big mistakes."

"But your family seems so stable. I assumed your parents had a good marriage."

"Depends on what you call good. They have the kind of marriage you're after. Passionless, but amicable. Not that I'm looking to lay blame—they did devote their lives to making mine the best it could be. But I've wondered at times if my problems in the relationship department weren't rooted in being the center of attention growing up."

"I wonder what's on the tube." Chris reached for the remote. Beating her to it, Greg knocked it to the floor.

"Anyway, I don't think that's healthy for a kid. They can end up real selfish people who don't know how to put someone else's needs above their own. And what comes of those who build their lives around a child who'll eventually be gone is a pretty sad thing to witness. My mother treats my old bedroom like it's some kind of a shrine. Hell, Dad says he can hear her talking to me like I'm in there and—"

"Enough."

"And there's something wrong with that. Why isn't she talking to him instead of a memory who picks up the phone when guilt kicks in? They don't have anything to say to each other, that's why. The only thing they had in common is gone, and some great job he's done so far with his own life, right?"

"Damn it, Greg! *Enough.*" She lunged from his lap. He heard the soft whoosh of her breath as his chest came down on hers, his weight pinning her to the floor.

"Wanna hit me, Chris? Go ahead, take your best shot if you want to shut me up. You're not doing Audrey any favors by hooking up with some man who doesn't love you enough to demand more than a mockery of a marriage. Is that what you want to teach her—better to feel too little than too much?"

"Stop," she whimpered.

Stilling her with fingers wound tight into her hair, Greg savaged her mouth until she returned the force of his hunger.

"That's it," he whispered roughly. "That's it, babe. Caring enough to fight and then to kiss and make up, that's what kids need to see. They learn a helluva lot more from two people who have soul between them than a couple of emotional strangers who happen to sleep together could ever teach.''

Chris went limp beneath him. She felt as if she'd been pummeled with a stinging truth, her emotional cowardice shoved into her face and down her throat.

His palm was on her throat, fingers stroking her jugular. How easily he could break her neck with a single snap of his powerful hands. *Greg had killed.* The thought came from nowhere, but she suddenly realized she was staring into the same eyes that had no doubt looked much the same as if he'd committed murder. Murder in the line of duty, but murder nonetheless.

His was the look of a man who sympathized with his victim but felt no remorse for the course of action he was compelled to take.

''You are merciless,'' she whispered.

''I am.'' Slowly he lifted his chest, sat astride her hips. From her vantage point on the floor he seemed larger than life, a skyscraper of a man, made of tough muscle and possessing a will of steel. From her throat to the opening of his shirt she wore, he drew down his hand. Eyes like the pinpoint sear of a laser burned into hers as he gave a fierce jerk.

The sound of buttons stripped from thread filled her ears and she felt the cool lick of air on her bared breasts. Greg reached for the tray filled with vegetables and scooped a celery stick into the brimming bowl of creamy avocado dip.

''Green, such a suitable color,'' he murmured, painting her nipples with dabbing strokes. ''Green as spring grass after a cold and lonely winter. Green with jealous envy. I'm jealous, Chris, jealous of any man having you except for me.'' As his mouth descended he warned softly, "A lesson to remember, babe. You're about to find out just how merciless I can be.''

CHAPTER FIFTEEN

CHRIS WORRIED HER bottom lip as she fingered the envelope Greg had slipped her after "dropping by" shortly before noon.

He hadn't stayed more than thirty minutes but it had felt like hours. Agonizing hours of polite chitchat with her mother and what seemed to be an inordinate amount of attention lavished on Audrey. The little girl who had done a quick about-face once Greg had told her she was the reason for his visit.

She'd gobbled it up, as if starved for attention. Never mind that Mama had poured it on her all morning, trying to placate a conscience working overtime. Chris hated paper dolls but Audrey loved them, so play with them they did. Audrey wanted to go to the park, so to the park they went. No matter it was cold and Chris wanted to be inside instead of chafing stiff fingers and paying her penance with each push of a swing. She'd done everything except buy jelly beans.

Those, she'd planned to buy this afternoon but Greg had saved her the trip. Well, Chris thought with a huff, maybe Greg could fool Audrey into thinking he was a "super-cool dude," but she knew better. He was a super-smooth stud who was trying to convince both child and mother that he was something he wasn't: Daddy material. Good thing she knew him as

well as she did, or Greg might have fooled her, as
well. He'd actually gotten on his knees to say goodbye to Audrey and give her a high five.

Audrey had giggled as they slapped palms, then
had thrown her arms around his neck. Standing protectively close, Chris had heard her whisper, "Do you
like kids?"

Greg's resounding, "You bet I do, and I especially
like you" was accompanied by a challenging smile
shot at Chris.

Just remembering it had Chris grinding her teeth
while her throat tightened all over again. She couldn't
deny that she was almost as touched as she was furious with the man. That Greg was trying to move
their relationship into deeper waters was obvious. But
even if she could shore up the guts to give them a
chance, it couldn't possibly work. Greg wasn't paternal; he was a strategist and she was his target for
conquest.

For all his seeming sincerity with Audrey—and
perhaps he even believed it himself—the bottom line
was, he was using a child to manipulate the situation
to his advantage.

"Oh, Greg." Chris sighed. "If only you were less
of what you are and more of what Audrey and I
need." Glancing around her old bedroom, Chris tried
to imagine sharing such simple, domestic surroundings with him.

But when the vision came with surprising speed,
she discarded it just as quickly. Too risky to let herself even think such things. She was vulnerable and
he was dangerous. Greg thrilled to a challenge; win-

ning was the name of the game for him. And should
he win her, the challenge would be over.

Steeling herself for what was sure to be an assault
on her defenses, Chris opened the envelope, fully expecting a love letter minus the gush. Sappy wasn't his
style.

And neither were love letters, even minus the gush.
His script and the message she read were as bold as
the man himself.

Several packages will arrive this afternoon. I
want you to wear the items I've selected just for
you—nothing else beneath the wrap, please. A
limo will pick you up at five and deliver you to
my requested destination. Expect an evening of
the unexpected. Till then, might I suggest a nap?

A nap!

Somewhere in the back of her mind she heard
Greg's low laughter. He knew very well that even if
she was dead on her feet she wouldn't have a prayer
of sleeping after this. Which only made her flounce
onto the bed and bury her head in a pillow. By golly,
she'd take a nap just to spite him!

Ten minutes later, Chris gave it up. No use, her
stomach was churning in anticipation. And apprehension. What game was he playing? What adventures
might the night hold? And *what* had he bought for
her to wear? Nothing else beneath her coat? Heavens,
what if he'd sent a merry widow with fishnet stockings and spike heels? And if he had, would she be
brazen enough to meet his challenge and wear them?

The sound of the doorbell had Chris racing for the

door, certain that Frederick's of Hollywood boxes awaited and how in the world would she explain *that* to her mother?

With a sinking sensation she saw Rick accept the packages. Next to Anna and Don, her brother was the worst person to get a hint of the double life she was leading.

"These are for you, sis." He gave her a probing look.

Heart in throat, Chris claimed the pile of distinctively wrapped boxes with a breathless, "Thanks."

"Neiman Marcus. Hmm."

Hmm, indeed! She had to admit, whatever Greg lacked in paternal attributes he more than made up for in the ability to surprise and impress.

"I've gotta hand it to him, Chris, his taste in stores is right up there with his taste in women. But I can't help but wonder about his intentions. You're my sister and I don't want to see you get hurt."

"That makes two of us, Rick. Don't worry about me. I'm a big girl who's simply enjoying a whirlwind romance."

"And that's all it is for him, too?"

Chris shrugged. "Don't tell anyone about these, okay? I'd like to check it out without an audience."

"Sure." Rick caught her arm as she turned. "You know, I never thought I'd play the devil's advocate, but a man does not go shopping at Neiman's for a woman unless he's after more than a whirlwind romance. Like the saying goes, the bigger they are the harder they fall. I think I hear a timber going down with a really big crash. Just something you might keep in mind."

"I do." Boxes piled to her chin, Chris took off, perturbed that Rick had spoiled her enjoyment with a guilt trip. She had enough of that to deal with already as a mother without adding her lover to the emotional heap.

Of course she didn't want to hurt Greg. And as long as they abided by the rules they'd agreed on, he'd be fine and so would she. She'd have to remind him of that tonight.

And then she'd have to put her foot down about any future visits with Audrey. No more steamrolling his way into the carefully orchestrated life she'd put on hold for a week, period. That was that and if he didn't like it, then...

Then they'd both be better off calling it quits now. Before either of them got hurt. *But could you do it, Chris? Could you walk away tonight without a backward glance?*

The question haunted her as she unwrapped the smallest box and found—

Stockings. But not just any stockings. A black seam up the backs with rhinestones circling one ankle; silky and transparent, they slid through her fingers like a French kiss wrapped in a whisper.

Eagerly opening the second package, she caught her breath.

A lacy black chemise with tiny jet pearls embroidered over the bodice joined stockings on the bed. Nestled in delicate paper beneath she found a matching garter belt.

No panties.

Lord, it was wicked! Absolutely the most wickedly gorgeous lingerie she'd ever seen.

Two boxes left and Chris allowed her imagination to romp naughtily. Perhaps a sheer black cocktail dress, split up either side to the thigh, lacy garters and hose tops peeking coyly through? Or maybe a black leather miniskirt with a next-to-nothing top?

With visions of decadence dancing in her head, Chris pulled off the lid and gasped, amazed to discover a flowing peasant dress, the fabric velvet, the design a collage of vibrant red roses and rich purple irises on a background of black. The hem zigzagged in a scarf effect from knees to mid-calf; the neck was scooped, the see-through sleeves sheared in graceful tatters like flag strips circling a Maypole and cinched at the wrist. Even the sash was a work of art: a length of supple black velvet with a mingling of purple and red silk tassels at the ends.

Holding the dress to her, Chris waltzed to the vanity mirror. It was a magical dress, unlike anything she'd ever seen before. And the woman she saw in the mirror seemed transformed by the magic it worked. Her eyes were Mona Lisa mysterious and her face had a rare glow, the sort of illuminated flush people had when they were in love.

In love? Chris shook her head, hard. Given that she most certainly was not in love and had absolutely no intentions of inviting such foolishness, she could only assume that the dress had a good dose of fairy dust sprinkled on it.

Moving quickly from the mirror, she shook out the dress. This was not reality, she sternly reminded herself. It was a waking dream, no more. After all, only in a dream would she open the final package and stare in awe at the contents.

A purple velvet cloak lined in black satin, with a voluminous hood. And a pair of matching ballet slippers. But it was the grace note she found, a single line on a piece of folded paper, that took her breath away.

See yourself as I do—Greg

This was how he saw her? Chris gave in to the luxury of imagining she was worthy of the compliment. An elegant, sensual woman who could inspire such enamored praise from a worldly man like Greg.

The problem was, she was playing a secret fantasy role in the fantasy world they had spun, one that had about as much real substance as cotton candy.

Chris stroked the velvet cloak. What little remained of her prudent nature advised her to return the packages to Greg and explain the gift was deeply appreciated but too expensive to keep. A lot like him.

Still, she couldn't resist at least trying on the ensemble. Gazing in the mirror, Chris could only think she did see herself as Greg did. At least for now, and now was all that mattered. She'd worry later about accepting such an outrageous gift from a man who brought jelly beans to her little girl and made a woman want more than anything to live happily ever after in a fairy-tale world where cotton candy was meat-and-potatoes real.

CHAPTER SIXTEEN

IT WAS A CALCULATED risk. Gloves off, screw the rules, he was invading her turf.

Chris wouldn't like it. At least not initially. Then again, one look at that plane ticket to Lubbock, and she might have tossed it into the trash, then hightailed it back the way she'd come.

But he didn't think so. If nothing else, she'd hop the plane just to order him off her front porch before the neighbors got curious. Which they already were, judging from the blinds lifting across the street. He was in clear view, the porch-light timer having clicked on shortly before.

Greg waved. Down the blinds went.

The swing that needed a fresh coat of paint creaked in the crisp evening air as he continued to rock easy on the home front; soon to become the front line.

Spying the headlights of the stretch limo he'd assigned pickup duty to, Greg took a deep, bracing breath.

And grimaced. Cow shit. Jeez, how could Chris stand smelling the stuff? He'd lay a thousand to one that the only reason she lived in Lubbock was because she'd met her husband at Texas Tech and his job and family had kept them here.

How...predictable. And safe. A whole grand world

awaited and here she was, rutting her life away. Too bad D.C. took three times longer to reach via air; he could've gone at this resident turf problem the opposite way.

He watched the back door fly open a second after the driver put the limo in Park. Yep, those neighbors of hers were getting an eyeful now. The driver getting out, Chris telling him to wait, and, as instructed, the driver taking off despite her frantic "Stop!" followed by a four-letter-word shout that pretty much described the air.

Cloak flowing, Chris looked like a queen marching up the cobblestone walk. A very pissed-off queen, to be exact.

All but stomping her slippered feet over the steps and onto the smooth pine porch, she stopped and glowered down at him, demanding, "What are you doing here?"

"Swinging. Care to join me?" he asked, patting the space beside him.

"No. No, I do *not* care to join you."

"Then why don't you ask me in? I'd like to see how the dress fits and it's a little too chilly to take off the cloak out here. By the way, it looks dynamite." Actually, so did Chris. Not only was she red-hot gorgeous, she looked about ready to explode. Hooking a thumb across the street, he slyly added, "I'm sure the neighbors agree."

Ruby lips pinched tight, she promptly rummaged through her purse, cursing softly until she dug out the elusive keys. Jamming one into the front lock, she gave a neat kick when the door stuck to the frame. The bottom needed planing. Greg wondered how many other odd jobs needed to be done around the good widow's house. He'd take a lot of pleasure in seeing to them. Maybe Jerry would, too.

Just the thought of another man leaving his mark on Chris's domestic domain had him clenching his jaw. It got tighter when she flicked off the outside light, as if hiding him and her traffic-stopping appearance from view.

"Well?" she said sharply, tapping her foot. "Are you coming in or not?"

In answer, Greg continued to swing, the metal link's *creak-creak* piercing the charged silence.

With an exasperated sigh, she huffed her way over. "So? What is it you want now?"

"Not much, really. Just the same politeness I'm sure you'd extend to any other guest. That is, anyone but me."

"What did you expect? You came here knowing full well how I felt about—"

"Defiling your home and reputation with my presence?"

"I never said that!"

"No, but the way you're acting says plenty. You don't want anything to do with me outside a rented room. I hear ya, Chris. Loud and clear."

She was quiet for a while. When she spoke, her voice was subdued but not exactly calm. "I think you're being very unfair about this. We had an understanding, and you're the one who's pushing to change the rules that were your idea in the first place. They were smart rules, Greg."

"I thought so at the time. But I didn't count on you getting in my head and running roughshod over just about every working organ I've got pumping in my body.''

"This is getting too complicated," she whispered.

Greg noticed she didn't worry her ring finger despite her obvious distress. He took some consolation from that.

"Yeah, it is getting complicated," he agreed, getting up. Palms on her shoulders, he stroked the velvet that felt as soothing as Chris did when he buried himself inside her. "Personally, I'd like to simplify things. How about you?"

"No argument here," she said, pulling away slightly.

Cinching his hold, Greg chose his words carefully. He didn't want to run her off by coming across as desperate and demanding as he was beginning to feel.

"I want you to acknowledge me. Maybe not as a permanent fixture. But couldn't you at least accept us as more than lovers? I consider you a friend, Chris. A very special friend who I care about just as much out of the sack as in. Don't shut me out just because the sex is good."

In the moonlight, he could see her tight swallow. Was she hesitating because she knew as well as he did the sex was good—hell, incredible—because of the emotional chemistry they generated? The irony of it was, those emotions she was so afraid of were the very ones that turned her on.

"I... Let's go inside and talk, okay?"

"Should I take that to mean the welcome mat's out?"

"For now it is" was her evasive reply.

"Good enough." *Like hell.* Keeping that last

thought to himself, Greg followed her inside. She turned on the overhead entry light, a small stained-glass fixture that gave the foyer a warm, rosy glow.

As she went about lighting up the adjoining living room and smoothing out a vintage shawl draped over a Duncan Phyfe couch covered in aged brocade, Greg smiled. Her home was just as he'd pictured it.

Except for the wedding picture prominently displayed on an old upright piano.

An urge gripped him to smash the frame onto the wood floor and tear the picture into a thousand mangled pieces. Damn, but he'd never felt so threatened before. And jealous. God, he was eaten up with the little green monster. Better get that smile back into place before Chris saw. *Do it,* he ordered himself. *Fast.*

His lips straining with the effort, Greg said, "Nice place. It's got your signature all over it."

"It's home. Make yourself comfortable and I'll see if there's some wine left in the fridge."

"I'd rather have hot chocolate if you've got some."

"Hot chocolate? Um…no problem." Truth was, he wanted Scotch, a stiff one, but cocoa set the mood he was after a lot better.

Chris turned toward the kitchen and he swiftly came up behind her. She stiffened when he caught her arms.

"Greg, please, I let you in to talk, not to—"

"I just wanted to help you out of your wrap, not get into your pants." *She didn't have any panties on.* Just a chemise and a garter belt holding up a pair of silk stockings. Sweet Jesus, he was suddenly so stiff that he hurt. The ache intensified to near agony as she slipped out of the gift he'd taken a gamble she'd accept, and pivoted.

"Thank you," she said stiffly. "I've never owned anything so beautiful. You're very thoughtful, Greg."

Thoughtful? He'd let her think so. But the gesture was more selfish than not. He had wanted to dress her with his money, cover her from head to toe as if she were his most prized possession.

"My pleasure. But Chris, you make the dress look great, not the other way around."

In Chris's gaze he saw a keen delight mingle with a kindling of arousal. Despite herself, she wanted him. Too bad for them both, he had no intentions of doing more than fanning the flame.

"I'll go make the chocolate."

"Want some help?" The quick shake of her head caused him to laugh wryly. "Don't tell me a man in your kitchen is more intimidating than sharing a toothbrush."

"In your case, only about double. If I know you, you'd wrestle me for the apron and probably organize my shelves after checking out the magnets on my refrigerator."

"Got some of Audrey's artwork displayed, do you?" Her wary expression confirmed it. "Relax. I know better than to push my luck in that direction tonight."

"Thank God for small favors," she muttered, heading toward the kitchen.

Watching the provocative sway of her hips, Greg endured a moment's masochistic pleasure before turning his attention to setting the trap.

CHRIS LET GO A SIGH of relief once she sensed his eyes were no longer devouring her retreating back. In the kitchen she tried to calm herself with the familiar surroundings, touching this and that. All was as she'd left it. And yet, she felt strangely removed, as if she'd departed the owner and returned a back-door visitor.

The water put on to boil, Chris gripped the tiled countertop's edge and leaned her forehead against a cabinet door, seeking their inanimate strength.

Finding none there, she smacked her fist against the countertop and paced the kitchen's length. *Damn him.* Damn Greg for weaseling his way into her home. Hard as it would be to leave behind those places they'd marked as theirs, at least she wouldn't have constant reminders around her. But she had to come back here, live here, and remember that his physical presence had once filled her home.

Would she ever be able to swing on the front porch again without thinking of him? And would she ever hear the rusty creak of the chain without hearing his plea for friendship, spiked with pride and demand?

He had no right, no right whatsoever to steal the peace she would desperately need once their affair was over. If he'd really wanted to be a friend to her, he wouldn't have done that, and she didn't think for a minute that Greg didn't know exactly what he was doing.

Much as she hated confrontations, they were due one now. At least the memories she'd return home to wouldn't be sweet or happy or passionate. *Especially* not passionate. As for the desire he'd already stirred up with no more than a look and a casual touch, she'd just have to deal with it. Anger would help. He'd defused it too easily on the porch; she couldn't let him do that again.

Chris made hot chocolate for Greg and poured a generous glass of wine for herself. Girded herself with as much self-righteous temper as she could muster, she strode toward the living room.

Anxiety rose when she saw he'd shut off the lights and turned on the twinkling ones wrapped around the Christmas tree beside him. Crouched in front of the fireplace, he pumped the bellows as if he had every right to make a fire in *her* house with *her* wood, and use *her* tools to change the atmosphere from quaint to intimate and make it their space instead of hers.

"Here's your hot chocolate," she said briskly to his shadowed back.

"Thanks, babe." He looked up with a gaze as warm as the fire he stoked.

"I'm not your 'babe' here, Greg. I'm your friend, remember?"

"You don't sound too friendly to me. Seems I should have elbowed my way into your kitchen, after all."

"Why not? You elbowed your way into my parents' house to see Audrey today and bulldozed your way into mine tonight."

"Taking back the welcome mat, Chris?" He made a *tsk-tsk* sound of disapproval. "That's no way to treat a friend."

"I thought about it, Greg. We're not friends."

"No?" He stood and accepted the mug she held out. At her soft gasp, he smiled innocently. Her palm tingled where he'd flicked a fingertip before claiming the cup. Taking a sip, he licked his lips and Chris caught herself about to lick hers in response to the movement. "Ah, it's even better than Mom's. But don't tell her I said so. It'd hurt her feelings and I wouldn't want to do that."

Chris took a gulp of wine and immediately wished she'd brought the whole bottle.

"What about *my* feelings, Greg?" she demanded.

"Tell me what they are and I'll see what I can do about them."

"I feel violated, that's what. This is my house and Audrey is my daughter and that's what I've got to come back to in a few days."

"Don't you mean *all* you've got to come back to? Except for your job and your search for Super Dad, of course."

"That's right," she whispered fiercely. "It's all I've got and the last thing I need is you taking that away."

"Let me think about this." He left her standing in front of the fire and sat on the couch facing it, his posture a comfortable lounge. His gaze trained steadily on her, he sipped at his chocolate. "Why don't you sit with me?" he asked companionably. "Let's just sit and talk."

"I don't want to get that close."

"Because you don't trust me or because you don't trust yourself?"

"If you must know, both."

"That's honest and I respect honesty above all else. It's the thing I prize most about our relationship. Sure, I admit it, I've done my best to take advantage when I can, but I've been honest about that, too. As for yourself..."

He lingered over another sip and she silently damned him for looking so natural on her couch, for making her feel so ridiculously pleased he liked her hot chocolate better than his mother's.

"Go ahead and say it," she challenged. "Say that I'm a coward who'd rather lie about her feelings than admit them."

"Actually, I think you're doing a fine job of expressing yourself. Even if they're not what I want them to be, I'd rather you expose your gut feelings than hide them from me. But I wish...I wish I understood a lot of things better. Like your choices. Why, Chris, *why* would you rather go back to living a life you told me you hated and wanted to change, when I'm offering you an alternative that—"

"Stop right there." Chris held up her hand, warding off the seductive lure of his suggestion. "The only alternative is an on-again, off-again affair. When the nights get too lonely, a stolen weekend at some clandestine meeting place before we go back to our separate lives and—"

"Why do they have to be separate? Why couldn't we work something out so we could see each other once, twice a month? It'd give us a chance to see if our relationship's as dead-end as you seem to think, or if what we've got is as special as I believe it to be. Time would tell, Chris. Give us some time."

"I can't do that." She drank deeply, willed the wine to give her the borrowed courage she needed to stand firm. "I'm getting very tired of telling you this, so for once would you just listen. You don't have a child to consider, I do. Last night, you brought up some good points about what children learn from their parents. But they learn moral standards from them, too. If you came here, we'd end up in bed. Audrey would discover us sooner or later.''

''Probably.'' His pause was weighty and Chris felt the gathering momentum of a bomb about to be dropped. ''But by then, she'd surely realize that her mother was sleeping with a man for reasons other than lust. And as for that man, me, she'd know I care deeply for her mother. Who knows? In time, she might even decide, along with you, that I'm the perfect daddy for her.''

''No,'' Chris said emphatically. ''I want you to stay away from her, Greg. And after tonight—'' Her hand shook as she tossed down the remains in her glass. Almost choking on the words, she made herself say, ''After tonight, I want you to stay away from me.''

CHAPTER SEVENTEEN

CHRIS BRACED HERSELF for the hurl of his mug into the fireplace, the lover spurned to surge off the couch and oppose her with an eruption of fury.

But no, he simply put down his mug and tapped his fingers to his lips. Her own fingers wrapped so tightly around the glass it was a wonder the stem didn't snap.

"Okay," he said, shrugging slightly.

"Okay?" she repeated, certain she hadn't heard right.

"Sure. If after tonight you want me out of your life, gone I'll be. But you're stuck with me for—" he checked his watch "—a few more hours before the charter plane I booked leaves for Dallas. No commercial flights out that late, so you'll have to endure my company another hour there. You can take a cab if you don't want me to drive you to your folks'."

For a moment Chris was speechless. Nothing was as she had expected. Not the defensive words she'd heard come out of her mouth before she fully considered them. Not his easy capitulation. And not the horrible sinking sensation in the pit of her stomach.

The least he could have done was argued with her, fought for the two nights they had remaining.

Two nights she had thrown away.

Chris was suddenly as furious with herself as with him. She wanted those nights back. Desperately. But her pride was at stake, and backing down would mean she'd have to swallow it.

Even now, her pride demanded she strike back and incite the argument she wanted.

"So much for your future vision, Greg. You obviously hold as fast to potential relationships as you do to marriage."

"Hey, you're the one who insisted I drop it."

Not so much as an "ouch" his way. Unlike her, who wanted to pinch herself black-and-blue for saying what she'd programmed herself to think before weighing the consequences. And now she didn't even have a decent comeback.

"I shouldn't have accepted these clothes."

"Then give them back." He leaned forward, opened his palms; his gaze flinty, dark, it matched his challenge. "Go ahead, Chris. Take them off. Then put on whatever it is you wear in the role you play around here."

The role you play around here. Was it a role she played here? Or was it a role she was playing now, dressed up and acting out in a way she'd never imagined herself capable of?

Returning his level stare, Chris realized she wanted to hit him. She wanted to tear off their clothes and wallow all over the floor, bodies angry and hot, fighting each other for supremacy.

Who was she? What kind of woman was she to feel these primal urgings? And what kind of man was he to make her crave them? God, she didn't know. Greg made her so confused.

"I think that's the best idea you've had all night," she said unevenly. Yes, go to her room, put on her own clothes, wrap herself in the familiar and get some breathing space. It was absolutely the best thing she could do.

Chris took a halting step away from the fireplace.

"Where do you think you're going?"

"To my room. Alone." Alone, just as alone as she'd been there for years. For Greg to step a single foot inside her bedroom was unthinkable. "Feel free to read a magazine or something. I'll be back when I'm back."

"I don't think so." He pointed a finger to where she stood. "Here. You take them off here. In front of me."

"I can't do that!"

"Why not? It's not like I'm going to see something I haven't seen plenty of before."

That wasn't true, she wanted to rail at him. To bare herself here, she would be stripped of more than clothes. Here, she was so much more vulnerable than in a hotel room.

The scent of drying pine needles and woodsmoke mingled with the memory of hushed, intimate laughter. The memory slipped away before she could cling to its bittersweet hold. Greg's waiting silence was broken only by the sound of wood crackling in the hearth, the tap of her nails drumming the wineglass.

"I don't want to undress here because..." Chris took a steadying breath. "Because I don't want you to watch. And—and this is where I got pregnant with Audrey. Here, in this room, beside another Christmas tree."

"All the more reason, then."

"What do you mean?"

"Quite simply, you accepted what I gave you and now you regret it—apparently much the way you feel about ever getting involved with me. If you're shunning my gift, and us, I deserve to watch you do it. As for you, what better statement of independence could you make? Free from the past you kept yourself tied to, free from any ties to me."

Eyes narrowed, lips thinly smiling, he touched himself. A lingering stroke over his groin that made her belly draw tight and her fingers pulse with the urge to grip him.

"Don't worry," he said with a mocking chuckle, "I won't be taking this out or putting it in. So, go ahead, off with my clothes, on with yours."

When she hesitated, he snarled, "Take them off! Goddamn it, do it now or leave them on and keep them. Where're your guts, Chris? Where're your guts to do one or the other?"

Goaded by his insinuation that she had none, Chris hurled the wineglass into the fireplace. The sound of its brittle shatter coincided with her cry of "You wanna see guts? Then look all you like and see them."

Grappling with the sash at her waist, her hands were shaking so hard that she wished fiercely for a pair of scissors to cut the beautiful binding in two. When it was finally undone, she flung the length of velvet at him. His gaze simmered with the same white-hot light she'd seen as he'd pretended to be a vengeful warrior tying her to four saplings.

But that was pretend and what she saw in him now,

what she felt in herself, was real. They were engaged in a battle of wills and she realized that Greg had employed yet another subtle maneuver to bend her will to his.

He wanted her naked. He wanted her to beg him to make love to her and then beg some more—for the two nights back. And he wanted her to leave in the clothes she had come in.

Oh, yes, she knew *exactly* what he wanted. Chris was disturbed to realize that for now, at this moment, they wanted the same thing. Minus the begging.

Chin lifting, back straight, she held herself with pride. Her gaze challenging, she watched the shift of his eyes to her hands as they slid over the swell of her breasts.

Taunting him, she stroked down the length of her body until ever so slowly she raised the hem to just above her knees. Holding it there, she stepped out of the slippers, lightly rubbing her legs against each other. Then she parted them.

She smiled upon hearing his muted groan and inched up the velvet with a procrastination certain to bring him to the knees she wanted him on. Chris counted three groans before she drew the dress over her head. And tossed it to his feet.

His eyes did not follow the movement. They were glazed, fixed on her open thighs.

She widened her stance and felt the fire's heat lick at the moisture of her own arousal. Never had she felt so glorious in the fullness of her own sensual prowess and feminine strength. And what triumph she felt in holding them over the man who had led her, challenged her, to discover this heady power within.

"Like what you see?" she asked in a throaty murmur.

"I..." Like it? He coveted it. Greg told himself not to watch anymore. Not the way she baited him with the caress of her palms to her breasts, the intentionally seductive removal of the chemise. And he had to be a glutton for punishment to stare ravenously at her fingertip touching once, just once, the peak of her cleft.

"What are you doing?" he demanded in a voice so guttural he didn't recognize it as his own.

"Only what you want to be doing to me." Her laughter low and sultry, she fanned open her lips. "I'll let you, Greg. *If* you promise not to do anything else...unless you ask first and I agree. Certainly not your style, I realize. But that's the rule and this game's up if you break it."

Jesus, he thought, the woman had discovered she held a whip. And what a fast learner she must be, bringing him to heel with the crook of her finger and without a glimmer of mercy.

Standing, Greg grimaced. He had a raging hard-on and it hurt like hell to walk the few feet it took to reach her. Strange that he towered over Chris, but she seemed as tall or taller than himself. Something had definitely happened to tip the balance of power between them. Maybe he could figure it out later. For now he could barely think.

"I didn't say you could touch me there," she whispered.

"I'm not touching you." And he wasn't. His palms traced her arms in a phantom caress, stroked without contacting the warmth of her skin, which gave way to the rise of gooseflesh. A current of energy so strong it was electric leapt between as over and around he passed his palms, bathing her back and breasts with the charge of kinetic sensation.

At her belly, he stopped, hovered. Unbidden, a vision filled his mind and pulled at his heart. Chris, her belly rounded and full, their baby growing inside her—testimony to the purity of passion, the destiny of two souls bonded, the miracle of life. And a new life for him, enabling him to prove himself worthy as a father, a man who was committed and would never stray from his mate, his lover.

Greg swallowed hard. The vision was pure torment, just as Chris was standing there, enticing him with all the possibilities and refusing him access, eluding his every attempt to have and to hold.

Forcing himself not to grip her to him, he cupped her pubis and finger-stroked her with the delicate maneuver he knew she responded to best.

Several minutes passed and Chris was breathing erratically when she faintly protested, "I said you could only touch me there once."

"It's still once." Deepening his intimate massage, he pointed out, "You didn't mention any time limitations."

"All the same, I think you're cheating."

What did he have to lose? Taking the risk, Greg said with conviction, "I would never cheat on you, Chris. If that's part of what's holding you back, let it go. I'm not the man I used to be. And you're not the woman you were a week ago. We're good for each other, so damn good."

A sad sigh mingled with her moan. "We're good together in bed, Greg, but we can't live there."

She moved against his hand while unzipping his pants. When she dipped inside to release him, he caught her wrist.

"I said I wouldn't be taking that out."

"You're not. I am."

On a breathless little catch, she added, "I want you to come." But rather than feel subjugated by her whim, he found a transcendent freedom in the searing jolt of release.

Through slitted eyes, he had watched her wield the control he had given her over his body, elation rife in her smoky gaze as she exulted in that power.

Power was addictive, as he well knew. Chris had liked it, and, strangely, he was excited by her discovery.

She released him and Greg dropped to his knees. He pressed a lingering kiss to each interior thigh, then lifted his head and whispered, "Whatever you want, it's yours."

"I...I want those two nights back."

"Done."

"And I want to keep the clothes you gave me."

"We'll forget you ever wanted to give them back." The fire cast a warm glow over the garter belt and her skin. "Anything else?" he prompted.

Her gaze veered to the Christmas tree. Voice soft and tremulous, she said, "Make love to me with your mouth."

"Here?" Knowing that she had conceived Audrey in this very place, he was somewhat amazed by her slow nod. As he took her his amazement gave way to a secret triumph.

Chris believed she was conquering the significance of this room, and he supposed she was. But what she had failed to consider was that her objective was made possible by creating a memory as indelible as the first.

Their memory. One he filled with such heart and heat, he knew she could never erase what they'd shared beside this tree. And unlike a discarded evergreen, memories were for keeps.

CHAPTER EIGHTEEN

DRIVING AWAY FROM THE hospital, Greg was still smiling. He'd been visiting his sister daily. Her delivery had been a difficult one but she was bouncing back from the emergency C-section.

Glad as he was of that, he knew the smile he couldn't wipe off his face was owed to the cute little sucker that wet on him every damn time he volunteered for diaper duty.

Despite his initial hesitation to do much baby holding, he'd found himself becoming increasingly eager to cradle the infant in his arms and coax a tiny hand to wrap around his finger. His sister had teasingly said that his off-key singing was sure to give the baby gas, and after several loud toots that left them both laughing, he'd reluctantly handed over his nephew for a feeding.

Though he'd seen her nurse his twin nieces years before, and felt awkward enough to excuse himself from the room, his current reaction was different. It was a beautiful sight, the most nurturing and pure vision a human could ever behold. It had moved him deeply. Hell, he'd even had a lump in his throat.

Maybe that's why he'd decided it was time to leave and had offered to take his nieces for the day so his brother-in-law could spend some alone time with his wife and newborn son.

But he'd no sooner gotten Laura and Stephanie buckled into the back seat and driven down the street than they started to squabble over the doll both insisted they had brought along.

"Hey, double trouble, either hand that thing here or quit your fighting and share." Arm over the seat, he snapped his fingers, then opened an "I mean business" palm.

All immediately quiet, he glanced back and saw the doll nestled between the five-year-old twins.

The hell he couldn't be a good father, Greg thought. King Solomon couldn't have handled them better himself. Deciding to try out his paternal skills, he said, "Good behavior deserves a reward. How would you girls like it if I took you to the zoo?"

That won him a duet of 'Goody, goody' and a rise in his confidence. It rose amply for him to entertain a sudden idea.

Acting on it before he lost his nerve, Greg took a roundabout route that had Laura saying in dismay, "I thought we were goin' to the zoo."

"Me, too," Stephanie joined in. "This is the way to Grandma and Grandpa's."

"Not quite," he hastened to assure them. "I thought we'd swing by another grandparents' house. I know a little girl who's visiting there, just about your age. Let's go see if she's home and wants to come along." Their enthusiastic response helped steady the limb he was going out on.

Chris had been adamant that he steer clear of Audrey but she couldn't make too much of a fuss in front of three little girls over a simple invitation to join them at the zoo. Still, as he took the twins like so much arsenal to the front door, Greg knew he might very well be courting her protective wrath.

"Hi!" Audrey greeted them with a grin. The coat she had on implied she'd either just returned or was about to leave. Hoping greatly for the former, Greg stooped down and picked up a mitten she had dropped.

"I brought some new friends for you to meet, Audrey." In the midst of introductions, Rick appeared behind her and Greg stood, bracing himself for a repeat of sparring directed at his character and intentions.

"I hope you don't mind, Rick, but I was just passing by and thought Audrey might like to spend some time with my nieces since she doesn't have any playmates around."

"Hey, that's great." Rick offered his hand and his friendly man-to-man grip was as surprising as his chuckle when the small glove wedged between their palms. "Glad you caught us. It's just Audrey and me hanging out today and we were headed for the zoo."

"What a coincidence! So were we." Coincidence? More like heaven cutting him a break. "Care to make it a fivesome?"

"Sounds good to me. What do you think, half-pint?"

Both men's gazes followed the three girls racing each other to the car.

"I think that's a yes," Greg said, not bothering to hide his grin. It faded as he asked, "Where's Chris?"

"She just left with Mom and Tammy. Audrey

didn't want to go along and just between us, I think she's about to OD on her mother's TLC. Anyway, they talked Chris into clearing out some clearance racks. My guess is at Sears...not Neiman's.''

Caught off guard by the silent question in Rick's raised brow, Greg awkwardly cleared his throat. "Only the best for the best," he slowly replied.

"That's good enough for me." Rick gave an approving nod.

It wasn't like him to ask another man for advice or reveal his deeper feelings, but this was Chris's brother and a potential ally. Hard as it was, he told it like it was.

"I, uh, wish Chris felt the same way. I care about your sister, and not just a little. Unfortunately, she doesn't think I'm cut out to be more than a...a—"

"Fling?" Rick bluntly supplied.

"That's not what it is to me."

"If I didn't think so, I would have stepped in before now. Not that I wasn't tempted after Chris kept tiptoeing in at two in the morning and Tammy let me in on her whereabouts once I sweet-talked it out of her."

"Chris actually told her where we were?"

"Mother hens never go anywhere without leaving a number in case of an emergency."

Greg felt a mixture of discomfort and satisfaction that their private sanctuary was sibling knowledge. "I don't like sneaking around as if there's something to hide. There's nothing shameful about my feelings for Chris and if I had it my way our relationship would go way past a hotel door."

"She should know better than to be there but I've

gotta give you points for taking her to one with some class.''

''She's a class act,'' he said, quick to defend Chris. Seemed to him that Rick disapproved more of his sister's behavior than he did the man who was responsible for it. Greg didn't like that. ''She's also a grown woman who can make her own decisions without needing her brother's approval.''

They exchanged a level stare until Rick chuckled softly. ''You're looking better and better to me, Major. In fact, you're starting to look so good, I'll give you a little tip. Audrey's the one you really need in your corner. She's got a lot more clout with her mom than me.''

''So I figured. Dropping over to see Audrey wasn't exactly accidental. I want you to know that I appreciate you letting me have some time with her.'' He glanced at the car and waved back at the three little hands motioning them to hurry up. ''But in case you're not aware, I've been put on notice that Audrey is off-limits for me. Chris doesn't want her to form any attachments that aren't guaranteed to stick. She's not going to like it when she finds out I spent the afternoon with her daughter.''

''Unless you tell her, I see no reason why she has to find out. A word to Audrey from me and she'll keep quiet—she likes secrets almost as much as bubblegum jelly beans.'' After a pause he added, ''By the way, you get points for those, too.''

As they walked toward the car, Rick went on to say, ''My sister's a good woman, Greg, but as a mother she's overly protective. I think losing her husband is what's made her a little obsessive about keeping Audrey safe. It's a blind spot of hers, so try not to take this back-off thing with Audrey too personally.''

"But I do. I take it very personally, Rick."

"If I were in your shoes, I'm sure I would, too." The slap to Greg's back was one of commiseration. "Tell you what, while we're at the zoo I'll keep an eye on your nieces and give you a chance for some one-on-one with Audrey."

"I owe you for that."

Two hours later, Greg decided he owed Rick big time. As he took a lick of the ice-cream cone Audrey had insisted on sharing, he tried to remember when he'd ever felt so completely accepted and just simply *right* with a child.

He couldn't draw any comparisons because there were none. And Lord knew, nothing could compete with those adoring brown eyes staring up at him, the wistful little voice saying, "Gee, you're big, just as big as Superman. I bet if you wanted, you could touch the clouds."

His heart squeezed even as his chest puffed out. She made him feel like Superman; and what a rare feeling that was, almost believing he could leap buildings and take to the sky, exalted there by the wonder in a little girl's eyes.

Greg stretched high, then shook his head. "Seems I can't quite reach it. But maybe you could." Leaning down, he opened his hands. "How about it, sweetheart? Want to try?"

Audrey was in his arms faster than Superman could change in a phone booth. Over his head she went with a giggle of delight as he said, "Up you go on the top row!"

She rode on his shoulders until it was time to leave and it was with regret he gave up her slight weight to buckle her into the car seat while Rick did the same with the twins.

"That was a great ride, even better than a Ferris wheel. Thanks lots." For such a little thing, Greg decided Audrey packed a punch with her hug. Fact was, he felt like a fist had landed in his chest when she whispered in his ear, "I sure do like you. Please make Mama let us be together again. I can't ask since Uncle Rick told me this was a secret visit and Mama's not s'posed to know."

"I sure do like you, too, Audrey," he whispered back. "And I want more time together just as much as you. But I can't make any promises. The problem is, your mother... Well, she loves you an awful lot. And she seems to think it would be better for you to get close with someone besides me."

"But I don't want somebody else. I want you. I think you'd be a super-great da—"

"Shh." Greg laid a silencing finger against her lips. Pulling slightly away, he willed himself not to turn from the confusion and hurt in her soulful brown gaze. Only a child would be so open, so disarmingly honest. And only a heartless adult would abet a child's hope for a dream that reality could shatter. He couldn't do that to her; no more than he could let Audrey think he was rejecting her, as obviously she did.

"Listen, sweetheart," he said gently. "These things take time to happen, just like your teeth growing back in, and that means we have to be patient. Just remember that no matter what, I think you're very, very special, and anyone who could have you for their little girl is the luckiest person alive." Greg pushed back the pale, fine hair from her forehead and softly kissed her there. "Okay?" he asked.

"Okay." The spark of determination he saw told him that Audrey wasn't going to give up easily. *Good.*

"Then give me a high five." They slapped palms and in that brief joining he felt an uncanny sense of alliance, a connection that bound them in a shared cause.

As he drove, Greg noticed that the twins' animated chatter emphasized Audrey's silence. He glanced in the rearview mirror and their gazes met. She grinned and he wondered how long she had been watching him; if his unguarded expressions had revealed the turmoil of his thoughts.

Reaching over the seat, he patted her knee. Audrey caught his hand and squeezed it.

If Chris didn't break his heart, Audrey would.

Their destination reached, he helped her out of the car, intent on making a fast getaway before she got to him more than she already had.

"Thanks for a great day, Audrey," he said, playfully tousling her hair.

"It was the best," she pronounced. "And so are you."

God, how he wanted that to be true. But the fact simply was, he wasn't the best. He was only a man wanting to be the best he could be, a man who had fallen in love with a woman who doubted him even more than he doubted himself. A man who could easily love the child whose unconditional belief in him almost made him believe it wasn't misplaced.

Almost. Greg shook his head. "I'm sorry, Audrey, but I'm afraid there are better people out there than me."

"That's not true!" she protested.

"How do you know?"

Her little arms went around his legs and she looked up at him as if he were some great god in the sky.

"'Cause when I was on your shoulders, I touched the clouds."

Greg couldn't get any words out and so he lifted her up and let Audrey imagine she touched the clouds once more while he pretended he was Superman a little longer, just for the space of time it took him to deposit her at the front door.

A quick hug and he was out of there. Halfway to the car, a clamp on his shoulder stalled him.

"Hang in there, man."

"Yeah," Greg gruffly replied. "Thanks for everything, Rick. It was, uh…it was a really special day."

"And not just for you. Here, I've got you something to remember it by."

Greg took the small mitten that Rick held out, clasped it in the haven of his palm.

"Thanks, I'll consider it my good-luck charm."

Quickly, he drove away from the house he would return to in a few short hours and pretend along with Audrey that something wonderful hadn't transpired between them.

It had been so hard to leave her, yet he'd left with so much more than he had come with. Greg knew he had given something to Audrey, as well. Himself. The best of him, buried so deep he hadn't known it was there until she had dug it up with the ease of a child building a castle from sand.

The image of a wave hitting carefully piled white grains came at him and he could see the castle's threatened devastation.

Chris was that wave. Or rather, it was her consuming need to protect, her fear of allowing herself to love again.

Greg's jaw tightened. He couldn't make her love him. But intimacy was a doorway that could lead to emotional journeys and weaken defenses.

Tonight, he determined. Tonight he would push that door wide open. If Chris knew what was behind it, she'd surely slam it shut and run for safety with the speed of light.

And so, he'd entice her inside as he had before and once she was in too deep to escape, he would take them to a place where defenses had the substance of tin soldiers on straw ponies.

They wouldn't stand a prayer of surviving. Not when he could cut a path to her heart with the ultimate weapon: intimacy. A very unique expression of it. One that would strip away all barriers and lay their souls bare in a sexual arena where few lovers would ever dare venture.

CHAPTER NINETEEN

WHY HAD SHE AGREED to this—this crazy bedroom game? Was it because after tonight there would be only one remaining and she wanted to sow as many wild oats as she could before living out the rest of her straight-and-narrow days? Or was it because she'd developed a taste for adventure, the arousing hint of the forbidden in a dangerous liaison?

He hadn't touched her once since picking her up and already she was aroused. It was as though the absence of his touch made her want him that much more.

Perhaps that's why she had agreed to the fantasy he had requested—a fantasy that smacked of the forbidden. Yes, danger was in the air, invading her senses with the visceral thrill of a risk. Odd that she was a little scared but felt a sense of security, too. Maybe it was because of the password.

Roses. Chris's trust in him was ample to believe he would stop if she said, "Roses." *Why hadn't she cried "Roses" in her living room last night, or screamed it at the top of her lungs later, in her bedroom?* No matter that his lovemaking had been so tender it had bordered on sweet, why hadn't she called him off when reality had been ten times more dangerous than this exotic fantasy?

She squinted to better see the dark rider, all shadows and shifting movement in the unlit suite. Only they weren't in their motel room, either.

"Tell me where we are," he softly commanded, his voice holding a note of some secret mystery. And much of it was a mystery, their given roles to unfold as they went. All that was certain was the simple muslin blouse and long, full skirt he had brought for her to wear, a complement to the fantasy setting and century they were to pretend they were in, and an oil lamp, the only prop. As for the other item—she suddenly found it difficult to talk.

"Tell me where we are," he repeated. There was a hypnotic quality to his whisper. "In what time are we living?"

"It...it's the late 1800s."

"Yes. Now I want you to describe our surroundings."

"We're in a stable, near the Mexican border." When he remained silent, she took it as her cue to draw the setting in their minds. "It's a large, fine stable filled with riding gear, sacks of oats, a long row of stalls. A few are empty but most are housing purebred horses. Arabians, I think."

"Arabians, yes. Most are quiet now, since it's dark. A few are moving about, a little disturbed by our presence, but their movements are muffled by the hay under their hooves. Fresh bales are stacked near us. Can you smell them?"

She sniffed and imagined she could, that and more. "I smell clean straw. And leather. A storm is brewing and the air, it's heavy with the earthy scents around us."

"Earthy," he murmured. A match flared and illuminated his shadowed face as he held it to a cigar. Their eyes met and what she saw in his was both compelling and ominous. He shook out the match, cloaking them once more in darkness except for the glowing red tip that caught and held her gaze. She wasn't sure if it reminded her more of a warm, glowing coal or a single, glittering serpent's eye.

"Do you mind the cheroot?"

"No, I don't mind. The smoke, it's...faintly sweet."

"And so is your cologne. Tell me what else you smell."

"You. Even from here, I can pick up traces of sweat and leather—" *and lust* "—and rain. You've just ridden in after an extended time away."

"Nearly a year. Such a long time to travel abroad and leave my ranchero in the care of an elderly father and a foreman. Your older brother, *bambina*. The two of you were orphans and my family took both of you in as children. Now, tell me why I was gone. I'll hear it from the young woman who was the reason I left."

"You left because—because you no longer thought of me as a sister, not since that night you found me at the lake, naked in the water." Lucia shivered. Yes, Lucia was her name. And she was eighteen now, nearly an old maid by current standards.

"You were angry with me," she went on. "I remember you throwing my clothes at me, saying, 'Put them on, Lucia. What were you thinking, coming here alone after dark? A stranger could have found you, done something terrible to you. Put on your things, damn it, and don't ever let me find you like this again.' I remember you turning your back but stealing several glances while I dressed. I was shaking. But it wasn't from the night air on my wet clothes.''

"Then what was it?'' he asked in a silky whisper.

"You seemed like a stranger. A stranger who had found me and wanted to do something unspeakable to me.''

"Most unspeakable, Lucia,'' he assured her. His draw on the cheroot, a brightening red circle, seemed to concur with his carnal desires. "You were only sixteen and there I was, a man of twenty who had knowledge of harlots and brothels. The acts I suddenly wanted to commit with you, no proper woman would do. And you were not only proper, you were like my kin. But after that moment, I never thought of you as a sister again. You were the water nymph in my dreams and I damned you each time I woke up with my sheets soaking wet. Finally, I couldn't bear to see you and not touch you.''

She laughed softly, accusingly. "And so you did touch me. You gave me my first kiss. In the glade beside the lake, it became our meeting place. You fondled me there. And it was there that I offered you my virginity.''

A moment passed before he said, "But I refused.''

Why? she wondered. But then the answer came; she knew it because she knew him. Honorable though he was, he was equally selfish in his need for absolute possession.

"Yes,'' she agreed. "You refused. You said it was your fault things had gotten out of hand and it was for the best that you leave. I begged you not to go but you did.''

"If only you'd been a woman who knew her own heart, I would have stayed." The regret in his voice gave way to a startling anger. "Did you actually think I didn't notice how you flirted with the shopkeeper when I took you to town?" he snarled. "And those boys at the church social, the barn-raising dance, God, what that did to me. You were trying out your feminine wiles and the hell if I was about to risk getting you with child when you were still such a child yourself. So, tell me, who have I come home to?"

In her uncertain silence, he snuffed out the cigar with an agitated grind. "I'm waiting, Lucia. Tell me if I've come home to a fickle girl...or a woman who had the sense to wait for a man who would gladly give his life to protect her."

Of course she would have waited for a man as mature and fine as he, she started to say. But something held her tongue. Resentment, she realized. Resentment of the desertion that in her innocence she was responsible for. And he was a lusty man; had surely kept intimate company with other women while she cried herself to sleep at night, lit candles and said prayers for his safe and speedy return.

Oh, yes, she resented this man for awakening her desires, then leaving, forcing her to realize that the suitors who had come to call were callow boys, their kisses chaste and passionless.

"Wait for you?" she taunted him. "Why would I waste my time waiting for an arrogant old man—or should I say, stud? You do smell a bit like one, sniffing the tail of a mare who finds you not the least bit appealing. Perhaps if you took a bath I could tell the difference between you and these horses in their stalls. But you'd best be quick about it. A lover awaits and I'm already late for our rendezvous.''

''Who is he?'' His demand was so sharp, so harsh, she jumped. But he couldn't see the apprehension sure to be etched in her face, nor sense the delight she took in his jealous response. Toying with him, she said nothing.

''Answer me, damn it!'' The sound of a match struck roughly against a boot's sole gave way to the rattle of a glass chimney. Moments later he was bathed in lantern light. His countenance could have been that of a demon risen from hell, the blue-white light flickering over him, flames from the nether world he'd sprung from to exact a frightful vengeance.

Indeed, she felt the tug of fear. Danger was near. *He* was the danger. Tearing off the white riding shirt he wore, the expanse of his chest terse and awesome, he bore down on her, raw virility personified. His paces, measured and slow, the crunch of hay, the nicker of horses filled her ears.

She told herself to run, quickly, to hide herself in the night from this familiar stranger in black breeches and high leather boots. But she couldn't move, couldn't force her gaze from him.

Or the riding crop he tapped into his open palm. She'd never seen one quite like it—thin leather strips, perhaps a foot in length, dangling from the tip, both exotic and menacing. Two halting steps back she took, and he advanced at a leisurely stride that was somehow more threatening than if he'd lunged. His was the walk of a man who was confident in his just retribution. And her inescapable fate.

Whatever it might be, she knew in her heart he would never truly hurt her, his jealous rage no match for the tender emotions he bore her. And so, she tilted her chin up, faced him with the arrogance of his most prized and spirited steed. The one only he could ride. Bareback. For not even he could break it of its unwillingness to accept a bit or a saddle.

The tips of his boots nipped her bare toes. Glowering down at her, he growled, "What man has claimed what was, and is, rightfully mine?"

"Ask me no secrets and I'll tell you no lies." Her eyes slitted catlike and she licked her lips—only for them to part in a startled O at the crack of the tassels whipping the air. The slow shake of his head, the light tap of the crop against her thigh, gave her to feel she was in the presence of a strict taskmaster who regretted his wayward charge was in dire need of a lesson to remember.

"You have been a very bad girl, Lucia. But fortunately for you, I am a fair man. I'll forgo the punishment you've earned on two conditions. First, I want to hear you say that you love me and will never betray me again. And then, I'll have your confession. Five

words—'I was a bad girl.' All or nothing, you know that's my way. It's your choice, *bambina*."

His stern whisper carried over the air. How far was she willing to go to mend the damage done before they did more? That was the real question, and one she couldn't possibly answer to his satisfaction. Or hers. Compassion for them both competed with an urge to rebuke him for putting her in such an impossible position.

No, she would not tell him what he wanted to hear. Even if it might hold some truth, putting aside the past wasn't that easy. And besides, if she obeyed, he would become the man she knew and she rather liked this dominating side of him.

"No, I won't say it."

A poignant disappointment flickered in his gaze before he swiftly disguised it with a look of stoic resignation. With a heavy sigh, a weary shake of his head, he stroked the dangling leather over her breasts.

Her nipples beaded and her pulse tripped madly at the certainty of his purpose as quietly he said, "Very well, then, prepare for a punishment as naughty as yourself. Bend over."

She did not cower or cringe, but defied him with challenge clearly etched in her face, posture and voice.

"Make me." She laughed seductively.

"Ah, Lucia, when will you learn? That just earned you a worse spanking." He grabbed for her and she slapped at him. But now it was he who laughed. A foot taller and a hundred pounds heavier, he was smug in his superior strength. He captured her hands easily, bound both wrists with a single huge fist, the other holding the crop which he brought down smartly on her thigh when she aimed a knee between his legs.

"I said, bend over." The whip brushed her neck and he twined hard fingers in her hair. His tug of it was amazingly tender, yet firm and brooking no contention.

Her head pulled back, his breath was on her, smelling of smoke and lust, and mingling with her own halting gasps.

"Mind me and I'll take that into consideration. I can be generous." He rubbed her hip with the source of his generosity and she felt a scintillating sensation spread through her womb, expanding and making her greedy for the fulfillment of his threat.

But suddenly he let go, allowing her to fight him again if she so chose. He would like that, she knew; a struggle would amuse him, further distend his already rampant arousal.

It was a subtle retaliation, and she was sure he wouldn't forgive it easily, to acquiesce rather than scratch and bite as he so dearly loved her to do. Her senses pitched to their keenest measure, she could almost taste the pithy sob of defeat when she succumbed to the sweet lash of his whip.

"I am not a bad girl," she sniffed, coy in her disdain. "I'm a good girl, and you're a terrible man to spank me when I am so well behaved. Obedient I will be, but no matter how hard the strike of your rod, never will I give in to you."

His mocking chuckle naysayed her vow, as did the teasing whisper of the leather on her backside once she'd turned. Heart beating fast and furious, she heard the sound of his belt hit the hay-strewn floor, the thud of heavy boots discarded, the shift of his movements as he rid himself of the riding breeches. And then she felt the grip of his hands on her skirt, pulling it over her head, taking the muslin blouse along with it, and tossing them the way of his things.

"Widen your stance," he whispered. Though her legs had begun to shake, she did, and felt his knees nuzzle the backs of hers. Guided by the gentle pressure of his hand, she lowered her head and was rewarded with his approving murmur, a word of coaxing instruction. "Bend your legs...that's good. Your palms, cup your knees with them." His body heat lapped achingly near and a fine quiver of anticipation took hold. "Are your eyes closed?"

"Yes."

"Open them. Look on the floor and see what you find while I give you what you've asked for. By lesson's end, you might even discover your heart. You've wounded mine, you know. It's lying there at your feet."

She fixed her gaze on their silhouettes illuminated by the lantern and was held in thrall by the play of shadow and light. His palm slid over and down her belly, then lower to sweep once, twice, light fingerlicks that knew just how to stir and make her need.

And then she felt it, the insistent but miserly push of male invasion. When she instinctively bore down, he countered with an equal withdrawal.

"So compliant," he murmured. "Perhaps I was wrong and should spare you the rod."

"No! No, I deserve it. I am the bad girl that you say."

"Shame on you," he scolded her in a low, sharp whisper and dealt her the first velvet stroke of the leather. Hardly more than a brush, he mated it with a small thrust. "But more the shame on me if I don't make you see the error of your ways. Such a pert little ass you have, saucy as that mouth of yours that has a tendency to talk back. Only, you're so quiet now...not even a choice name for me? Or is it that you realize no other man could ever care for you the way that I do? One confession made, are you prepared to make the other?''

At his slight withdrawal, she instantly said, "Bastard. You cocky bastard—" and moaned in delight at the teasing sting between her cheeks, the feel of him entering her with such stunning force she lost her balance. But there were his hands, steady on her hips as he slowly eased out to where he had been before.

"'Cocky bastard,' is it? So far I've been lenient. Too lenient, I believe. Take back what you said, or you'll have to suffer the consequences for your disrespect.''

"Never, you son of a—" Her breath rushed out at the caress of his thumb. Then came several light lashes, the twist of his wrist applying equal chastisements to either side of her bucking derriere as he began to hump her in earnest.

"You bad girl. You beautiful, wicked girl. You deserve this for making me love you, need you, and refusing to love or need me back. Sweet Jesus, you're wet. At least you need this much from me. Need it more…more. *More.*''

Even in the midst of his furious possession, some part of her mind wondered how much of his avowed love and need was fantasy, how much was truth wrenched free in the heat of the moment. But the heat of the moment was such, she didn't care. She felt loved, consumed by the magnitude of it, as his mad rutting kept time with the delicate dance of the whip.

Suddenly, she winced. A single snap laid a stinging path across her buttocks and she cried, "Roses!"

Immediately, she heard the whip hit the floor. Just as immediately, he gentled his thrusting.

The password spoken, Chris was sorry to end their game and yet she was stunned by the wonder of the bond she felt with him. It was intimacy beyond her comprehension. A shriek of release formed in his name won his ultimate generosity.

He felled her to the ground and, with a lift of her hips, pressed until she was full of him. Buried inside her to the hilt, she felt his kisses to her hair, heard his ragged groans as he came and came.

Ecstasy gloved by ecstasy, his chest slumped against her back. Her cheek to the floor, her eyes wide open, Chris stared at the silhouette of their joined shadows while the red mist of unbridled passion slowly receded, amazement and confusion stealing into its place.

She didn't understand what had happened, but it was something subtly momentous.

"What have we done?" she whispered.

Greg rolled off her, cradled her in his arms to share the aftermath of a savagery that was strangely bitter-sweet. He knew what had happened. And though he hadn't won the war, he'd gotten a fair share of the spoils he'd been after.

"You feel good tucked against me like this." Better than good, she felt perfect. Stroking back her hair, he kissed her softly, soundly, then whispered, "Did I hurt you?"

"No. Except for the last one. It stung."

"When I heard you yelp, I was ready to get rid of the crop before you could say 'Roses.' I'd never hurt you for the world. Tell me you know that, Chris."

"If I didn't believe it, I never would have agreed to the fantasy." She went very still. "It was a fantasy, wasn't it?"

"Yes and no. We did what we did and now it's part of who we are."

"But what did we do? You didn't answer me when I asked, but I get the feeling you know something I don't."

"I think I do." Slipping off the condom he had loathed to put on, Greg wondered how much he should say. This was terra incognita for her, but in lots of ways for him, too.

"Well? Are you going to tell me or not?" she pressed.

"You know, babe, I like it when you get pushy with me. You've got that rare ability to go after what you want, once you decide you want it and not come off like a bitch. Just one of the reasons I'm so crazy about you."

"Greg…" she said in that warning tone he found irresistibly cute. He couldn't imagine a kid being sufficiently intimidated by it to straighten up and behave. He'd be good at putting his foot down, balancing discipline with a generous quota of back pats and hugs. Between him and Chris, they could make a fine team of parents; he just needed more practice like he'd had today. The only problem was convincing Chris.

"Okay," he said slowly, painfully aware of his limited time to do much convincing. "It was an object lesson. The whip, or cat, was the teaching tool—for both of us. What it *wasn't* was a kinky bit of S & M, because that's shallow. What happened between us goes a lot deeper than that. We discovered magic."

"Magic?"

"Magic and more," he confirmed. "Your trust in me had to go beyond the ordinary and my protectiveness toward you had to be greater than my desire. The game was a means to an end, a search for a deeper intimacy than most people are comfortable with. I wonder...has this left you feeling uncomfortable or disturbed?"

"A part of me says that's exactly how I should be feeling, but..." He felt her head shake a "No" against his chest, the fan of her breath there as she confided, "But that's not how I feel."

"Tell me," he whispered.

"Close. So very close to you. I guess if anything disturbs me, that's what it is. And to tell the truth, it's beyond me how something so...sexually beyond the pale can seem so emotionally holy."

Holy. To hear her say it, what hope it gave him. She was quiet for a while, but then he heard a catching little sniffle. "I—I don't think I'll ever be able to see a rose again and not remember this."

"Good." He tilted her face up and brushed aside a single tear. "And while you're at it, remember something else. We don't just have sex—we have sacred sex." Swallowing hard, he forced himself to say the hardest words he'd ever said in his life: "When you get back to Lubbock and go in search of that father you don't think I can be, it might be a good idea for you to sleep with another man or two."

Her expression stricken, she said, "How can you talk about our sex being sacred in one breath and push me toward another man's bed in the next?"

"With great difficulty, that's how. It's agony for

me to even think about, but I figure it's the surest way for you to realize that what we've got together, no other relationship could ever compete with.'' He touched her cheek and she turned away.

"Greg. I want you to stop."

"Only if you say the password."

Her watery gaze meeting his, she whispered, "Roses."

CHAPTER TWENTY

"OH, MAMA, PLEE-EASE? Please let me have it." Audrey looped her arms around the big stuffed giraffe standing guard at the toy-store entrance.

Chris glanced at the price tag. "Sorry, sugar. It's way out of our price range. Let's go in and see what else we can find for the trip home tomorrow." Her voice caught on the last words. She didn't want to think about it. If she did, she'd totally humiliate herself by giving in to the tears she'd been fighting all day.

"Okay," Audrey said with a sigh. "Maybe we can find some colors and a colorin' book—one with mommies and daddies and flowers and stuff."

Mommies and daddies and flowers and stuff. Chris wasn't sure what bothered her more—Audrey's mention of "daddies" or her easy acquiescence to forgo what she really wanted. She was such an obedient child, so eager to please. Chris had always thought it a positive quality, but now she wasn't so sure. Life could be hard and kids who didn't know how to fight back were at a disadvantage once their overly protective parents weren't there to tough out their battles for them.

God, she was starting to think like Greg, she realized. Damn him, anyway, for putting such ideas in her head. Audrey was perfectly fine just the way she was. Sure, she needed a father, but her mother's love life had no bearing whatsoever on the provision of a stable home. Audrey had to come first, just as she always had, no ifs, ands or buts about it.

Shuffling through a pile of coloring books, Chris pushed aside one with a family on the front, a little girl wearing a big frown and the mother holding a newborn just beneath the heading: Oh, No! A New Baby Brother—What About Me?

"Look, Audrey, here's one with Barbie. Let's get this one, okay?"

"Okay. But can I have this one, too?"

Chris silently groaned as Audrey flipped through the pages of the baby-brother book. And then she groaned aloud when she glimpsed the giraffe loping their way. Guided by none other than—

"Special delivery for Audrey Nicholson," he called loudly when Chris tried to hustle her in the opposite direction. "Is there an Audrey Nicholson in the store? Please come and claim your stray animal. He's loose and eating all the candy!"

"Look!" Audrey shrieked, breaking free from Chris's urgent grip and racing toward the giraffe that reared up in greeting. But rather than wrap her little arms around its neck, she latched on to Greg's as he bent down, smiling broadly. She gave a big kiss to the cheek Chris wanted to slap.

How dare he? How dare he waltz in and try to buy Audrey's affection? She was just an innocent little girl who couldn't possibly realize she was a bargaining chip in an adults-only game.

Marching over, Chris said sharply, "I'm sorry, Audrey, but you can't accept gifts from…from strangers."

"But he's not a stranger," she protested, tightening her hold when Chris attempted to reclaim her daughter. *Her* daughter, damn it. "He's your friend. And he's my friend, too. Aren'tcha, Greg?"

"You bet I am," he assured her, returning Chris's glare with a level stare. "Say, sweetheart, if it's okay with your mom, why don't you call me Uncle Greg? I'm not a member of the family, but I sure wish that I was."

"Me, too!" As Audrey turned Mark's somber eyes on her mother, Chris saw a spark of defiance light up her gaze. "I wanna call you that. And it's okay with Mama…Uncle Greg."

Chris silently counted to ten and told herself that after they left the store—minus the giraffe and the infuriating man who was now the proud owner of it—she would straighten things out with Audrey.

"Audrey…sugar. Mom wants to talk to her 'friend' alone for a few minutes. Why don't you go find a few treats to eat on the way home tomorrow? We'll probably be leaving in a rush and won't have time to stop on the way."

"Can Uncle Greg come with us?" Before Chris could grind out a "No," Audrey put the question to him. "Can you?"

"I wish I could, sweetheart. But I have to get on a plane and fly to where I live. It's a long way from here."

"I've never been on a plane. I've never been anywhere 'cept here and home. Know what? It kinda smells bad there sometimes. Sure wish I could go on a plane and way up in the sky where the angels and birds live." With an oddly secret smile, she added, "But most of all, I'd like to be in the clouds. So close, I could touch 'em."

Greg's smile was an echo of Audrey's as he tweaked her nose. "Tell you what, Audrey. No promises, mind you, but I'll see what I can do to talk your mother into letting you fly way up in the sky from your home to mine and get as close to those clouds as you want."

Audrey whispered something in his ear and he whispered something back. Straining to hear, Chris felt the bite of exclusion. She knew it was childish, but still she resented them sharing a secret that didn't include her.

Neither did she like Greg reaching into his pocket and plopping a load of change into Audrey's palm. And she liked even less the way Audrey scampered off at a single "Vamoose" from Greg, stopping to flash him a grin without sparing a glance her mother's way.

"Okay, she's gone," he said, rising. "Go ahead and let me have it, but try to keep your voice down to a low roar."

"What are you doing here?" Chris demanded between clenched teeth. If she gritted them much harder, she'd probably have two more missing than Audrey. "What are you doing here and how did you find us?"

"I stopped by your place and Rick told me where I could find you. Have to confess I watched you for a while, but I was enjoying myself so I waited until I saw a chance to make points with Audrey. Which is obviously the reason I'm here."

"Well," she huffed, "you certainly didn't earn any points with me. I can't believe you! You—you—"

"Cocky bastard?" He laughed smugly as her cheeks flared red. "What's wrong, Chris? Got some trouble dealing with your little girl hugging the man who put a whip to her mama's bottom the night before?"

"Damn right, I do. What goes on between us is strictly that and has no place tainting my relationship with my daughter."

"'Tainting,' is it?" he returned with a maddening control. "Funny, last night our tainted relationship was holy. Call me stupid, but I just don't get it. Why is it that you believe your intimate life has to be this separate entity that has nothing to do with anything else?"

"Because..." She searched for an explanation but couldn't come up with anything except it was simply how she'd always viewed it. Certain he'd shoot a hole through that reasoning, she said self-righteously, "Because that's the way it is and should be, that's why."

"My, but you sound sure of yourself. Just as sure as I am that nothing could be further from the truth. Especially since once you get hitched to... well...whoever, the two of you will sleep together, right?"

"Of course. But that won't affect Audrey."

"Oh, I disagree. While she certainly won't be privy to what goes on behind closed doors, her parents' private relationship is sure to affect the overall atmosphere at home. Especially if Mama's tense and avoids her bedroom at night. And she just might notice that Mama would rather kiss and hug her than dear old Dad.''

Lips thin, Chris said tightly, "I hate it when you do this.''

"Do what?" he asked innocently.

"Twist and turn everything around so that you seem right and I'm wrong. How you do it, I don't know. But you do it every time, damn you.''

Greg shrugged. "Hey, it's not hard. After all, I am and you are. Right and wrong, that is.''

Oooohh. Chris did a slow burn. Thumping the giraffe on its head, she demanded, "So, what are you going to do with this? Something tells me it won't match your decor.''

"No, but it'll look great in Audrey's room. And just maybe she'll think of Uncle Greg when she hugs it.''

"You can deep-six that idea. Audrey's going to be crushed when she has to leave without this bribe of yours,'' she snapped.

"It wasn't a bribe," he snapped back, his composure suddenly slipping. "I gave it to her because I wanted her to have it. And I gave it to her because— because I never spoiled Arlene like that. It's too late for me with her and this was my chance to see a little girl's eyes light up the way Audrey's did. And you know what? I loved it.'' His Adam's apple worked up and down. Before she could stop herself, Chris instinctively touched his hand.

"If you're dead set on Audrey not having my gift, so be it,'' he said, kissing her hand softly, then returning it to her side. "But Chris, you'll have to be the one to explain why she can't have what I gave her. This was my gift to Audrey, and hell can freeze over before I take it back.''

HOW IN THE WORLD did she end up carrying this thing while Audrey was perched on the "top row"—as Greg had called his shoulders? Chris continued to wonder this as she awkwardly shifted the giraffe through the madhouse, otherwise known as a mall.

"How about a bite to eat, girls?" In minutes, Greg and Audrey had decided on their choice in the fast-food court. While they ate and talked, seeming not to notice Chris's own absence of conversation, she again felt the nip of jealousy. Those two had something going and she wasn't in on it.

Suddenly Chris wondered if she wasn't falling victim to the same petulance Audrey had exhibited that day of their awful fight. *Grow up,* she told herself, *and be a good sport while you're at it. They're having fun and it won't last long, so don't spoil it for either of them while it lasts.*

Tomorrow she and Audrey would be gone.

And so would "Uncle Greg."

CHAPTER TWENTY-ONE

"SURE YOU DON'T WANT to see the New Year in with the revelers in the bar? There's quite a party going on down there and I could impress you with my knack for working a crowd."

Chris's chuckle was strained. "That's okay. I'm sure your social skills are just fine. Heck, if you can impress my brother and parents, the Queen of England probably wouldn't think twice about inviting you to dinner."

He patted his stomach. "I'm still stuffed. How about you?"

"After steaks with my folks and strawberry short-cake with yours, it'll be two days before I'm hungry again." Her own stomach growled, calling her a liar. Spending time with both sets of families while their own inevitable goodbye too fast approached had worn her nerves thin and eating had been the last thing on her mind.

"I, uh, I really appreciate you putting in an appearance for my mom and dad." Pulling her closer on the couch, he tucked her head against the crook of his neck.

Lord, but he smelled good. And the sound of his low voice, so strong and calming...dear God, how she would miss it.

"You know, Chris, they've been real curious about this old girlfriend I've been 'courting,' as Mom puts it. Hope you don't mind all those nosy questions she was asking you. I got the feeling you were starting to feel a little tense. Especially that last half hour it took to get out the door."

Chris mentally rolled her eyes. She'd thought they would never get away and escape to their suite. All that time with their families when they had next to no time left for themselves. Only good manners had kept her where she did not want to be.

"That's okay," she told him. "My family's just as bad if not worse. And besides, this is New Year's Eve and it was only right for us to spend at least a little of it with our folks. I think they were all pretty disappointed that we had plans to go to a party and couldn't share a toast with them at midnight." She pointed to the champagne bottle on the coffee table. "So, ready to party?"

"Ready as I'll ever be." When he turned her in his arms, their gazes met and she wondered if her own was as troubled as his. "But the truth is, I'm not in much of a partying mood. I'm feeling somewhat depressed."

"Me too, Greg. Me, too." She knuckled his jaw. "We're a sight, aren't we? Half an hour to the New Year and here we are, crying in our beer. Wanna make love? Maybe that would cheer us up."

"I'm not sure I can get it up just yet," he said. "If it's all the same to you I'd just as soon settle for some heavy necking and lots of snuggles, cop a few feels on the couch and—ah shit."

"Ah shit, what?"

"I forgot to pick up a box of rubbers. We used the last one last night."

"All the more reason to settle for some heavy necking and plenty of cuddles." Hugging him tightly, she said, "Actually, Greg, I'd rather end it that way. Just enjoying each other's company and not getting into an argument about where you want to go from here, I don't want to remember our last night as being spoiled by a fight. When I look back I'd like to think of how good it was just to be together."

"And how good it is, Chris." He kissed her softly, deeply. "Know what? You're the best company I've kept, ever. And I already promised myself that I won't spoil the night by rehashing our differences. You know how I feel about things and vice versa. We'll let it lie for now and I'll just have to gamble on distance making your heart grow fonder."

"It's plenty fond already, bug guy." Touching her nose to his, she gave him an Eskimo kiss. "Did I ever tell you how much I like you?"

"Not in so many words, but you've let me know in a thousand different ways. Like giving me half of your cheesy rags. If that's not love, what is?"

Love. He'd said it again, and not in the heat of a mind-bending fantasy. Chris ducked her head. She didn't want to think about that word and she didn't want Greg to use it. It tugged at that place she'd sewn tight that night in the car and had vowed never to let tear her apart again.

As if he sensed her feelings, Greg busied himself with the champagne.

There was no hurling of glasses into the mock fire-place, no ribald laughter or putting the bottle anywhere except on the coffee table as they saw midnight in with a toast. His simple "Here's to a new year as wonderful as the last week has been," and her, "Hear, hear" pretty much said it all.

After that, they talked about everything and nothing, hugged and kissed and fondled until his watch called it five.

"I should get you home," he said, looking seductively rumpled after all their cuddling on the couch. "You've always been in by two. Sure your family won't think I've totally corrupted you by keeping you out all night?"

"I told them it was an all-night party and we were meeting some old pals from high school."

Laughing wearily, Greg shook his head. "Seems I didn't do a good enough job of corrupting. That reputation of yours is still intact despite my best efforts. Except your neighbors are probably still talking about what happened on your porch."

"Let them talk," she said with a tight little laugh. Their time was up and they were actually leaving. Where was her breath? Why was it so hard to draw one past the constriction of her throat? And her stomach, it was so tied in knots that she'd surely throw up if she had any food in it.

Forcing herself to smile, she said brightly, "See? You have corrupted me, after all. I really don't give a damn about what old Mrs. Howard thinks. If she had a life, she wouldn't have to keep herself busy by sticking her nose into mine."

"Good for you, Chris," he said, pulling her up. Holding her close, all but crushing her to him, he whispered, "Good for you."

Hugging each other by the waists, they walked slowly to the suite's entrance. Greg opened the small closet where their coats were hung and reached inside. He stood there, just stood, his hand poised over the hangers. And then his fist smacked the adjoining wall.

"We can't leave it like this," he said hoarsely, breathing hard. "God, this is tearing me up, babe. It's tearing me up and—and—" He gripped her to him and she clung with an equal desperation. "What am I going to do without you? Jesus, I want you. I *need* you."

"Why didn't we make love?" she whispered, her hands frantic in their search of his chest, his wonderful, strong chest she'd never touch again. "We had all night and we didn't even take off our clothes. All that time and we wasted it talking, doing everything but—"

"It's not too late." His voice urgent, his palms just as urgent as they raced over her breasts with a fever to match her need. And kisses, hungry, eating kisses. His lips memorizing her face, their mouths clinging as she fumbled to release him from his pants, then holding him, stroking him, pressing his turgid flesh possessively against her belly.

"Be inside me," she pleaded while he gave up on pulling down her hose and ripped them with a fierce, savage yank. Her back to the wall, he lifted her up and she wrapped her legs around his waist.

Just before he pushed inside her, he said raggedly, "We've got no protection."

"Thank God. For once, just this once, I want to feel you without anything between us. It should be safe, my period's due in a few days."

"I'll make it safer and pull out before I come. Now hold me, babe. Hold me like you'll never let me go."

She held him as if her very life depended on it and her body accepted his fevered upthrust without resistance. She was wet for him, her womb starved and already weeping at the loss for what she had now. Again and again he thrust, each departure a painful reminder that her body would soon be empty of his presence—and so would her life.

Gripping him inside, and gripping his waist, his shoulders, Chris could feel her back hitting the wall, her head thrashing against it, the desperation surrounding them and closing in while she moaned his name, over and over. She did not want to come. Not her, not him; never did she want this to end.

She fought the inevitable as long as she could but all too soon her body opened up, then closed in a greedy fist around him where he pressed. Her hungry womb sucked at his tip and she bore down, instinct demanding he fill it. A cry of his name ripped from her throat. And then he was groaning, "Oh God, oh God," and jerking out of her.

Warm spurts on the inside of her thigh, Greg pressing hard there while she commanded herself not to force him back inside where they both wanted him to be.

His arms were shaking as he lowered her legs; neither of them capable of standing, they slumped to the floor.

"What's this?" he whispered haltingly, his fingertips trembling as they stroked her cheeks.

"I'm sorry," she said, a sob catching while the tears continued to ignore her demand to stop. Maybe if she said "Roses" they'd listen, she thought with a piercing sadness.

That only made her cry harder.

"Hey, it's okay, babe," he said, his voice a croon sweeter than a lullaby. "You just go ahead and cry until you're all cried out."

"If—if I did that then we—we might be here forever."

"That'd suit me fine," he said solemnly, and Chris struggled not to say that it would suit her fine, too.

It took a while for her tears to recede, but eventually they did. In silence they put each other back together. In silence he helped her on with her coat. In silence he handed her the empty champagne bottle with pretty pink flowers on it.

And in silence, they shared a parting glance at the room filled with the memories they had made. Then left arm in arm, never looking back after the final close of the door.

"I'M WORRIED ABOUT YOU driving home sleep-deprived, Chris. Can you put off leaving long enough to catch a few winks?" It was hard to talk.

"Actually, I'm pretty wired. Don't worry, between some coffee and the radio, we'll make the trip fine. And it's only six or so hours away." She touched his hand, which gripped and ungripped the steering wheel while the car continued to idle in her parents' driveway.

They sat there a few moments longer, neither of them seeming to know what to say. Heaven knew he didn't. But whatever it was, it sure as hell wasn't goodbye.

"I guess this is goodbye," she said, breaking the heavy silence. And then she offered her palm, sideways.

A handshake? She actually thought they could part with a handshake? Greg stared at her in disbelief.

"Don't you think that's a little formal, considering?"

Chris dropped her hand and wiped her palm on her skirt.

"What would you suggest? A farewell kiss?" Her small laugh was dry, brittle. "I don't think so, Greg. You know us. Once we get started, one thing leads to another and—"

"I love you, Chris." There it was, without warning, the one right thing to say. "You don't have to say you love me back, but I do love you and no matter what, I'll always be there for you. I'm as close as a phone call away."

"Greg, please. Please, don't do this. Don't make it any worse than it already is." She reached for the handle and he gripped her wrist.

"Marry me."

Chris wrenched her hand free. "This is horrible enough. Why did you have to ask me something like that when you know full well what my answer will be? I *can't* marry you!"

"Why not?" Damn, but he was losing it, losing the control he had sworn to himself he would keep. And here he was, ready to grovel, get down on his knees without a stitch of pride and beg her to marry him. The third time would be the charm, he wanted to scream. He wanted to yell at her that if she would only give him the chance, he'd prove what a good father he could be.

Screaming and yelling—yeah, that'd convince her, all right. He had to get out of here, get away from the beautiful, tormented face he was dangerously close to kissing senseless, roll down the window and get some fresh air into this car that was so crowded with raging emotions, he was choking on them.

"Never mind." Reaching past her, he flipped the handle and flung open her door. "Go on. Get out."

"Greg, I—"

"Goddamn it! You heard me. I said *get...out.*"

With a sharp cry, she lurched from the seat and ran toward the house.

He told himself not to watch until she'd gotten in safely. But he did. He told himself not to act like an asshole and peel out of her driveway. But he did. And he told himself that tears were for women, and men who cried them were weaklings, and strong as he was, he would not cry.

But he did.

CHAPTER TWENTY-TWO

THE ONCOMING MACK truck's blaring horn mingled with Audrey's scream and the squeal of tires beneath them as Chris swerved from the interstate's middle line and onto the shoulder.

Once the car had rolled to a stop, Chris gagged on the coffee and bile trying to come up. Grabbing Audrey to her, she assured herself they were still alive.

"Are—are you okay, sugar?"

"I—I'm scared, Mommy," she whimpered. "The big truck was coming at us and—and—"

"Shh, shh. Mama's sorry, so sorry." More than sorry, Chris was furious with herself. How close they'd come to being killed and it was all her fault. She should have been watching the road, not replaying that horrid scene with Greg in her mind. Just another sign that getting involved with him had been a lapse into temporary insanity and the sooner she put it behind her, the better.

What was done was done and now it was time to wise up, get her head back on her shoulders where it belonged. Thank God they were almost home. There, she could think clearly.

GREG EYED THE TELEPHONE in his kitchen. He wanted to call Chris and assure himself she and Audrey had arrived home safely. Chris had no business driving after staying up all night, and the state he'd left her in wasn't conducive to alertness on the road. If anything happened to them, he'd never forgive himself.

He picked up the phone. Put it down.

If he called, she'd surely hang up on him. But he'd go crazy worrying about them. He picked up and dialed. After five rings he was ready to hop a plane and go in search. On the sixth ring, she answered with a breathless "Hello?"

Her voice washing over him, he forced himself to say, "Sorry, wrong number."

CHRIS REPLACED THE receiver with unsteady hands. Still shaken from the near miss, she wondered if the raw edge of her nerves had made her imagine Greg's voice. Covering her ears, she screamed in silence, tried to drown the echo of *"I love you.... Marry me.... Get out."*

A tug at her arm caused her to look down. There was a wealth of insight in the somber brown eyes peering at her.

"What the matter, Mommy? Are you missing Uncle Greg?"

"He's not your uncle, Audrey." Kneeling, she clung to the little girl who was her reason for living. The one who hadn't called her "Mommy" in years but seemed as needful of a security blanket as Chris was herself. "We'll talk about it later, okay? Right now, Mommy just wants to be with you. How about a cup of hot chocolate?" A vision of Greg with a cup of cocoa assaulted her. *Damn him.* Even something as ordinary as hot chocolate was riddled with memories.

"I'm not thirsty. Can I go play with Lizabeth?"

With difficulty, she let Audrey go. Out of her arms, then out of the kitchen, out of the house. Though her child was just next door, Chris felt deserted. She needed Audrey to keep her company, to give her a sense of order while inside she was coming apart at the seams.

And what comes of those who build their lives around a child who'll eventually be gone is a pretty sad thing to witness. Insidiously, Greg's words filled her mind. Her gaze fell on the cup he had sipped from, unwashed on the countertop. She lifted the cup and her lips hovered where his had been. Quickly, she grabbed a bottle of dish soap. Scrubbing furiously, she cleaned the cup, then put it in the dishwasher for good measure.

She had to do something, keep herself busy. Seeking to rid her house of his last traces, she mopped the kitchen floor he'd walked on, shoveled out the fireplace, took off ornaments and hauled the Christmas tree out to the alley's trash bin.

Needles pricked her and she was glad for the little jabs of pain; they took her mind off the far worse pain clawing for attention that she was desperate not to give.

She willed the vacuum cleaner to suck up more than dry pine needles, to inhale and devour the memory they'd made in the living room. And then bedroom. *Why had she let him in here? Why had she let him lie on her bed?*

It was still unmade from their lovemaking. Chris

jerked off the top sheet and flung it to the floor. But as she touched the bottom one, the one on which they had lain, she hesitated. And then she softly stroked the sheet.

A sob in her throat, her knees gave way. She threw herself on the bed and imagined Greg was there, holding her.

Hold me, babe. Hold me like you'll never let me go.

She had to find the strength to let him go. She had to wash the sheets that had touched him. Tomorrow. Tomorrow she'd wash them. But tonight she'd be weak and remember....

THE HOUSE WAS SPOTLESS, just as he'd left it. God, but it was like a museum around here, Greg thought. Funny, he'd never seen it that way, everything in impeccable order but a lack of warmth in the high-tech decor.

The place needed a woman's touch. Crocheted doilies covering up worn spots on some lived-in furniture, ugly panty hose draped over a towel bar, toys that got underfoot on the floor. What the damn place needed was signs of the living, sounds of laughter and even an occasional fight.

The silence around him pressed in and he continued to stroke the small mitten he held.

"Chris," he whispered, then, gripping Audrey's glove, he yelled, "Hey, babe, let's grab the kids and go get a bite!"

Yeah, lots of fun eating alone. Just about as much fun as torturing himself with visions of Audrey on his shoulders, a minivan, dirty diapers and coming home, roses in hand, to a frazzled wife.

He had to get out of here. Where, Greg didn't know, but anything was better than talking to the walls that didn't talk back and pacing through a house that was far from a home.

NEVER HAD CHRIS BEEN so glad to see Audrey off to school and get back to work herself. For the next eight hours she wouldn't have to field questions about why Mommy seemed so sad or why they couldn't go visit *their* friend. And at work she wouldn't have to remember Greg's visit with every room she entered, or the bed she had yet to change linens on.

But most important, at work she'd be too busy to think about the questions that assaulted her: Had she been too convinced of her own rightness and made the mistake of her life as a result? Could it be that he actually did love her in the ways that counted, lasted? And was it possible that she loved him just as much but was too afraid to admit it?

Quit beating a dead horse, Chris, she mentally chided herself as she poured a cup of coffee in the teachers' lounge. The answers were plain. Cutting things off was the wisest move she'd made since they'd met. And as for love, the kind that lasted? No way. A whirlwind affair did not a workable marriage make.

Marry me. The coffee lodged in her throat and Chris forced it down past the sudden lump there. She had to remember he'd asked two other women before and it must be force of habit, a weakness he had for buying into a fantasy, then wanting out once reality set in. No, she had no intentions of being another divorce statistic, nor of Audrey being a casualty of domestic war.

"The bell's about to ring, Mrs. Nicholson. Why aren't you in your homeroom? I've a good mind to report you to the principal. Or better yet, the assistant principal."

Startled, Chris whirled around and sloshed coffee onto Jerry's coat sleeve. "Oh, Jerry, I'm so sorry," she said, frantically grabbing for some napkins.

He caught her dabbing hand. "If you really want to make amends, say you'll chaperon with me at the school dance this Friday. I'll even throw in a corsage."

"I—I—" She couldn't get past the stammer, nor her gripping urge to turn him down flat. "I appreciate it, but—"

"Look, if you're worried about school policy, nobody has to know we're on a date. As far as anyone else is concerned, you had car problems and I gave you a lift. No big deal."

But it *was* a big deal, she wanted to tell him. It was a big deal that he obviously cared about the no-fraternization policy, and his PC mentality irked her. *Wait. Hold it right there.* What was she thinking? A week ago she would have been concerned about the same thing—their reputations and jobs dictating social discretion.

Greg again. Damn him, anyway. His influence was a bad one and she had to start thinking her way, not his. A date with Jerry, the most levelheaded person she knew, was exactly what she needed to get her feet on the ground where they belonged.

"What time should I expect you?" she asked, managing a halfhearted smile.

"Why don't I pick you up at five and we can have an early dinner. Someplace quiet, you know?"

Indeed she did. He meant someplace where they weren't likely to be seen and recognized. Distaste for such secrecy filled her and she felt a swift empathy for Greg and the feelings he must have had while she prattled on about her reputation and the sterling example she was compelled to set.

At the shrill sound filling the room, Chris could only think, *Saved by the bell.* Saved from her thoughts and making small talk with Jerry.

But as they departed the teachers' lounge, their date made, she found herself thinking more of what she oughtn't. Jerry had a fat butt. Chris blamed Greg for making her take notice of that. She'd never paid attention to a man's rear end until she'd hung over Greg's shoulder and realized what a work of art tight buns could be.

WORK. WORK WAS THE TONIC for all that had ever ailed him before. Only, after four days of work he was ailing worse than ever and he hadn't gotten squat done, even putting in time and a half.

Greg glanced at the clock on his desk. Nine on a Friday evening and he didn't want to stay any more than he wanted to leave. He couldn't sleep. He couldn't eat. And if he talked to the walls in his house much longer, they'd just maybe start talking back.

Clearly, he was emotionally and mentally in a place he'd never been despite his marital disasters. He wondered if Chris would have turned him down if he'd had a clean slate. Or did she think he was one of those Mickey Rooney types who hopped in and out of marriage like other people changed clothes? If she only knew how seriously he took it, his failures making his need to succeed so much more imperative.

Hell, he was a safer bet than that Jerry jerk who surely didn't have near his experience in damage control.

Jerry. Chris would have seen him by now at school and what hell it was wondering if she was seeing him for reasons other than work. And what if she slept with him, took the advice Greg wanted to cut his tongue out for ever giving? And what if they got a hold of a faulty condom or Jerry wasn't as careful as he was and Chris got knocked up?

Imagining another man touching her, putting the baby in her he himself had begun to crave, a red rage seized Greg. Struggling to control it, he asked himself if he'd love Chris as much, still want her for his wife, if she were to become pregnant with another man's baby.

Greg pondered that unsettling question and emerged with a telling realization. Were the baby an accident, he'd blame himself, not Chris, for it. And he certainly wouldn't blame an unborn child any more than he would Audrey for having been conceived. Yes. *Yes.* He'd love Chris just as intensely and still marry her in a heartbeat.

The only thing he wouldn't be able to forgive would be if she *wanted* another man's child instead of his. He'd had his chance to try beating the odds against her cycle and he hadn't taken it, knowing that was one strategy that would be wrong, wrong. But a part of him regretted he hadn't stooped to such ruth-lessness.

He'd felt the first jolt just as he left her. Replaying it again, he frowned, trying once more to remember if he'd exited before that initial spurt. At the time he'd been too obsessed with possessing her to record such a minor-yet-major detail. Ah, hell, it couldn't have been more than a drop, and though a drop was all it took to get pregnant, she'd said the timing wasn't right.

The phone rang. Grabbing for it, he prayed it might be Chris come to her senses and as senseless in love as he.

At the sound of Eileen's voice, his heart dropped flat and he damned himself for a fool.

After hanging up, Greg put his desk in order. At least he didn't have to spend the evening alone. And just maybe ex-wife number two would help him fig-ure out how to convince Chris she was meant to be wife number three.

"WELL, GOOD NIGHT, JERRY. Thanks for a great time." Great? It had been *awful*. Worse than awful, she'd never been so bored in her life.

Chris quickly amended that. As he kissed her, a kiss that was dry as dust on her end and way too wet on his, she wasn't sure whether she was more bored or disgusted.

Disgusted, she decided, when he slid a palm down her back and over her behind. Discreetly, of course, in keeping with his furtive glances around the restau-rant where he'd forgone a glass of wine and raised a brow when she'd ordered one and lit up. As for his careful survey of the bill and stingy tipping, she hadn't cared for them any more than his kissing and the butt handling that she put an end to with a quick step back.

He made a sound similar to the one he'd made when she had laid a five on the table for the waitress—one of disapproval mixed with a hint of embarrassment, as if he'd accidentally farted and turned an accusing glare on his dog. Greg, however, would not only claim such a fart as his, he'd probably rank it on a scale from one to ten.

There she went again, Chris realized with dismay. She'd been comparing the two men all night.

"Mind if I come in?" Jerry asked, clearing his throat.

She did mind, but made herself say politely, "Maybe another time." *Not.*

"Then I'll see you at church." With that, he left and Chris breathed a sigh of relief as she let herself in, paid the sitter, and went to check on Audrey.

She was sleeping with the giraffe, the huge stuffed animal taking up most of the bed's space. A wave of tenderness made Chris's heart soften and lurch as she remembered the toy-store exchange between Audrey and Greg.

Audrey had responded with such open affection that, despite her pique, Chris had been a little amazed. Her child was usually reserved with people she didn't know, especially men, and her ready acceptance of Greg was both extraordinary and disconcerting for a mother who thought she knew best.

But did she? He had been so good with Audrey that day. Chris saw that now, looking back with the clarity of distance. Could it be, she wondered, that he had some latent paternal qualities emerging to which she had shut her eyes, her focus narrowed to old, stubbornly held parameters?

A soft kiss on Audrey's cheek, a pat of the giraffe, and Chris went to her own lonely bedroom. For being so empty it felt awfully crowded. The walls closed in and she confronted the conflicts she could no longer ignore.

The answers she'd been feeding herself lacked the substance of truth. "No more lies," she whispered. "The simple fact is he's under your skin and has a hold on your heart. You made a mistake, Chris. A really big mistake. So, what are you going to do about it now?"

Marriage was a possibility, she decided. But they needed more time together, the three of them, to make such a binding commitment. Time was the answer. The distance between them would make things more difficult, but anything worth having was worth working for. Good marriages took work; they could think of it as a proving ground, a test of their mettle.

Chris felt as if a thousand-pound weight had been lifted from her shoulders, blinders lifted from her eyes. Elation and a lilting hope swept through her. She wanted to share it with Greg. Tell him how wrong she had been, ask his forgiveness for the wounds she had inflicted.

That, too, would be a test. True love forgave, and as with the birth of a baby, the pain was forgotten once a beautiful new life was cradled in one's arms.

And how she did want to be in his arms right now! The thought sent her heart soaring.

Chris cut her gaze to the bedside clock. Eleven here, it was midnight in D.C. Even if Greg was sleeping, surely he wouldn't mind if she woke him up to ask when was the soonest they could meet.

Rummaging in her purse for the card he had given her with home and work numbers on it, she grasped it with tremulous hands. Excitement rising, she dialed. Breath held, an immediate apology on her tongue, she heard his receiver lift.

"Hello?" It was a woman's voice. Into Chris's stunned silence, the woman said, "Major Reynolds' residence. Hello?"

"WHO WAS THAT?" Greg asked, looking up from the hamburgers he turned on the stove.

"They hung up. Wrong number, I guess."

Just in case it wasn't, he grabbed the phone and dialed. Better for Chris to hang up on him than to think he'd been in the sack with Eileen. Their relationship was too complex to explain easily, but he'd explain her away somehow if Chris had called.

Which apparently she hadn't. Ten rings, no answer. After midnight and she wasn't home. *Who was she with?* And who was baby-sitting Audrey, or was she at a friend's house while her mother was out on the town...or elsewhere?

Greg returned to the stove and slapped the hamburgers onto a plate, hard. Eileen scratched softly at his back.

"I take it she wasn't there?" she said sympathetically.

"You take it right." He shoved the plate her way. "Here, eat both of them. I just lost my appetite."

"Even for—"

"Yeah, even for that, Eileen. Like I told you earlier, I appreciate the offer, but I just can't cheat on her."

"It's not like you're married," she reminded. Again.

"No one knows better than us that there's a lot more to marriage than a legal paper. It's the 'lot more' between me and Chris that's keeping me out of a bed with you to try to forget her." At Eileen's expression of slight hurt and definite disappointment, he softened his rejection. "If anyone could tempt me that way, it would be you. But the fact is, no one's worth that kind of damage. Even if she didn't know, I would. And I couldn't live with that between us."

"I don't believe it," she said, shaking her head in disbelief. "It's finally, really happened to you, hasn't it?"

"God, has it. I'm crazy about her, Eileen. And I'm just as crazy about her little girl."

"Lucky them," she said wistfully. "I wish it could have been that way for us. But I suppose we should be glad that we've been able to stay friends and occasionally enjoy the best thing we had in our marriage."

"That part of it was good," he agreed. Spicy as their love life had been, though, it had lacked the depth and meaning that defined his intimate bond with Chris. Too private to share and better left unspoken to an old lover and ex-wife.

"I'm going to miss our little frolics down memory lane."

"Yeah, but you sure as hell won't miss the rest of the garbage that went along with our 'I do.'"

"Isn't that the truth," she admitted with a laugh. "Once the honeymoon was over and the domestic stuff got in the way of the bed... Well, I guess it's not too surprising we thought it best to keep the bed and forget the rest. Maybe I'll be lucky and meet a man one day who loves me as much as you obviously love her. Not that I'm in any hurry, mind you."

And he knew she wasn't. Fiercely ambitious, Eileen was married to her career. A lot like he had been before Chris and Audrey had come along and scrambled his priorities.

"Let's eat those burgers," he suggested. *Sonic burgers are my favorite.* He could hear her halting whisper in the elevator as if they were still there. The memory seized him in the groin and wrapped around his heart. Both belonged to Chris. All of him did. God, but he missed her.

"Tell you what, while we eat, give me an earful about this amazing woman who did the impossible."

It was all the encouragement he needed. As they ate, he told her about Chris, about the blind spot she had that made her refuse to give him a chance to be Audrey's daddy.

"I want them, Eileen," he said as she nibbled at the burger he hadn't touched. "More than anything I've ever wanted in my life, I want them both."

"Hmm." She tapped her temple. "Know what I think? If you're smart you'll give her some space, show her you can be patient. It's certainly not your strong suit, but if you can lay off the arm-wrestling tactics, she might start seeing you in a different way. I know that after tonight, I do.''

She gave him a quick kiss, then picked up her purse. ''Call me if you want to talk...or anything else.''

''There won't be 'anything else,''' he said firmly.

''I know. But you can't blame an ex-wife for trying.''

They laughed companionably as he walked her to the front door. There, he asked, ''By the way, how do you see me now?''

''You're not the man I married, Greg. But you're showing some real signs of being the one I wish I had. If that woman has a brain in her head and a hormone in her body, she'll come around. Just give her some time.''

As DAWN PEEKED THROUGH the blinds, Chris huddled in the fetal position on the floor of her bedroom. Disbelief had given way to outrage, a wrath she'd taken out on the phone she jerked from the wall, the sheets she'd shorn with her scissors.

And then the tears had come, unending streams of them, each one filled with the hurt wrenching her apart and leaving her in so many pieces, scattered and fragmented, she would never find them all. But now, mercifully numb, Chris knew she had no choice but to pick up what was left of herself and what remains she could gather, and put them in place as best she could.

She had to do it for Audrey. She had to do it for herself. She couldn't allow Greg to destroy her. All their memories and her tattered emotions, she had to tuck them away in a sealed place of her mind where she must never venture.

To church she would go Sunday and with Jerry she would sit. And she would look at him with the veil of self-delusion lifted. As for comparisons, he would surely fare infinitely better than Greg after this.

And he did. So did Harvey, whom she didn't hesitate to accept a date with the next weekend. Chris heard herself laughing at his corny jokes, struck by how natural she sounded when she felt so completely detached. She watched their interaction as if she were an onlooker, just as she went through her days at work and her time at home—with a sense of separation from everyone and everything.

Everyone except Audrey. Chris could feel herself clinging with such desperation it was enough to suffocate the poor child. She knew she had to stop it, and would as soon as she found a few more missing pieces. Rationally, Chris believed she was in shock—not unlike what she'd gone through when she had lost Mark. The symptoms were the same: going through the motions of living while inside she felt cold, dead.

Her period was nearly three weeks late, but that didn't really surprise her, either. She had skipped one entirely after Mark's death. Yes, she was a widow again, but she refused to grieve at the grave of lost dreams, lost hope.

It was only after the first week of February came and went without a sign of her menses that Chris became alarmed. Had she miscalculated? she wondered frantically, checking the last X on the previous year's calendar.

But no, there it was and no matter how many times

she counted the days, they didn't miraculously diminish. One period she could miss and explain away but the only explanation for having missed a second was inescapable.

The calendar fell from her nerveless fingers and her gaze riveted on her stomach. "Heaven help me," she whispered. Her surroundings zoomed in and out and she thought she might faint. Slumping to the floor she put her head between her knees and breathed deep until the dizziness passed.

But as reality reasserted its hold she wished she had fainted. *What was she going to do?*

Chris had no idea. She only knew that she was pregnant and the father-to-be would never know.

CHAPTER TWENTY-THREE

SITTING IN THE CLINIC'S waiting room, Chris's heart stopped, then started again when the name called was not hers.

She was desperate for this to be over; desperate for it not to happen. But she had no choice, she sternly reminded herself as she closed her eyes and searched for some remnant of strength. She wanted to pray, but she'd been praying for two weeks and God hadn't sent a miracle miscarriage her way.

She thought He would forgive her for what she was compelled to do if heaven's unconditional love was true. But self-judgment was another matter and Chris wondered if she would ever be able to forgive herself.

She believed life was sacred. Only she had been thrust into an impossible situation where beliefs and existing responsibilities collided. She had examined the options and outcomes as rationally as she could. This had been the hardest, most painful decision of her life.

To bear this child would be to subject Audrey to a fate she did not deserve. The taunts from her peers and inevitable snubbing they both would receive would only be a single thread in their unraveling lives. The structure that supported them was frighteningly fragile, Chris had come to realize. This was a moral community and her position in it would suffer a great fall. Her teaching contract was due to be renewed for next year and the school budget had been cut.

She could hear the clip of her job already. An unmarried home-ec teacher with her stomach out to there would incite an uproar among those parents who felt she was no example for their children to follow. Gone would be the income and gone would be the existing fabric of their lives.

To do that to Audrey was unthinkable. And so was climbing into bed with another man who might or might not marry her, even if she was able to convince him of a desperate lie.

Desperation had driven her here, where she shrank into her chair, into herself, while another name was called.

So desperate she'd been, she had actually considered calling Greg and insisting he marry her, take her and Audrey in until the baby was born. And after that they could divorce, she could return to Lubbock with both children and bear only the brunt of bad judgment for being swept off her feet by an old flame and jumping into a marriage that hadn't worked out.

It was really the most logical thing to do. But Chris didn't think she could survive living with Greg and the equal measures of love and hate she grappled with even now. Lord, how she wanted to hate him, completely and passionately. Yet there was a weakness inside her, making her wake up and wonder why he wasn't in bed with her. How weak she was, longing so much for his touch that she pretended it was him, the traitor whose name she called when she came. And then damned as she cried into her pillow, cursing him for the hold he still claimed over her body and soul.

Yes, she still wanted him despite the brutal damage he had done. And it was that want which advised her to stay far away because she would fall for him all over again and then he would tear out the remains of her heart.

"Mrs. Nicholson?" The call of her name was close, too close, and Chris started at the tap on her shoulder. The neatly dressed woman looked down at her quizzically. "I called your name twice but you didn't seem to hear. Is something wrong? The nurse is waiting with your prep shot."

Chris glanced from the woman to the open door leading to a nurse who would dope her up, to a room where she would lie on a table while her womb gave up the life inside it. And once that was done she would go home without the baby in the belly she protectively stroked, home in a cab rather than the car she had come in and would have to pick up later.

The car she was leaving in now.

"I can't do it," she said haltingly. "I'm sorry if I messed up your schedule but I just can't—can't do this."

The woman nodded sympathetically. "If you can't, then don't. After all, the only thing to be sorry for is going through with a decision you can't take back and regret once it's made. I'm sure that yours is the right one for you.''

And it was, Chris knew as she claimed the haven of her car and carefully drove home. Home with the child she hadn't been able to sacrifice for the sake of her other one.

She would have a lot of explaining to do. Why Mama was having a baby but didn't have a daddy to offer in the bargain. And why it was best that they move away after the school year was over and find a new home, new friends, a new job.

But she'd sweeten the deal and tell Audrey what a team they would be and wherever they lived it would smell lots better when they swung on the porch, sharing jelly beans, lullabyes and lemonade.

EIGHT IN THE MORNING and he hadn't slept a wink all night. His plane was due to leave in two hours and Greg was still debating whether or not to call first. He was having a lot of trouble making decisions lately; had been for the past three months. Good thing he wasn't running a war since he would have had a mutiny on his hands by now.

He was ineffective on the job and had been strongly advised that whatever his personal problem might be, he needed to get it straightened out. Hell, he hadn't needed the general to tell him that—all he had to do was look in the mirror for a reality check. Twenty pounds lighter, his eyes dull and sunken, on good days he looked like a zombie in a horror flick.

Maybe Chris would take one glance at him and

have some pity. Only, he didn't want her pity. He wanted *her*. On any terms. It had come down to a matter of survival.

Half an hour remained before he drove to the airport. If he called, she might make herself scarce. Then again, if he didn't, she might have Saturday-afternoon company when he arrived, as in male, and given the state he was in, Greg didn't trust himself farther than he could spit. If he made a scene, he'd blow what little chance he had for a reconciliation. Knowing that, he laid aside the mitten he'd rubbed a hole in from months of stroking, took a deep breath and made the call.

"Hello-wo," piped the pip-squeak voice trying to sound grown up. It was the most wonderful sound Greg had heard in what seemed forever.

"Audrey," he exclaimed with genuine delight. "Guess who this is."

"Uncle Greg!"

"That's right. How's my special girl?"

With a mischievous little giggle, she said, "Which one? Me or Mommy?"

"Both. But you first."

"I got a tooth in but lost two more and the Tooth Fairy only left three quarters under my pillow. Just 'tween us, I think Mommy's the fairy, but don't tell her I said so."

"Cross my heart, I won't."

"Does that mean you can keep another secret?" she asked in a confidential whisper.

"You know I can." Unable to resist, he asked, "Remember our secret at the toy store?"

"Sure do, but I was 'fraid you forgot."

"Nope," he assured her. "I think about it all the time. So, Audrey, tell me your secret before I talk to your mom."

"She's kinda the secret and I don't think she can talk right now 'cause she's throwin' up again."

Everything seemed to come to a stop. His heartbeat, his lungs, even his ability to speak. And then they came back all at once, faster than fast, the room spinning like a top.

Struggling to remain calm, Greg said very slowly, "This is really important, Audrey, so think hard before you answer. Does your mother have the flu?"

"I don't think so, 'less it's a real weird kind and lasts a long time. Mostly she's just sick in the mornin's and eats crackers in bed a lot."

Symptoms, other symptoms. Jesus, he couldn't think. "Uh...what about sleeping? Is she sleeping a lot, too?"

"Almost as much as she cries. I'm worried about her and that's my secret, Uncle Greg. She keeps tellin' me everything's gonna be all right but it sure doesn't seem like it. 'Specially since she said we were gonna move away after school's over and after that she has a surprise."

A surprise? Fourth of July fireworks and Mardi Gras in New Orleans exploding at his feet couldn't compete with this!

"Listen, sweetheart, don't you worry your pretty

little head a second longer. I'm on my way and I'm not leaving without you and your mama.''

"Is that a promise?'' she asked with such hope it assured him he had a formidable ally in Audrey.

"You bet it's a promise, no matter what it takes for me to make it come true. Between the two of us, we'll make our toy-store secret happen. You'll be calling me something besides Uncle Greg real soon.''

After swearing Audrey to silence and making her a fellow conspirator in a hasty plan, Greg took off, with the frayed mitten in his pocket for luck. Galvanized into action, he made two stops on the way to the airport and boarded, out of breath, his checking account considerably lighter.

A while later, arsenal in hand, he got out of the car he'd rented and breathed a sigh of relief when he saw Audrey posted at her station, right on time.

She ran into his arms and gave him a great big hug, the best hug he'd ever gotten in his life, almost crushing the foil-wrapped roses between them. He pulled one out and gave it to her with a warning, "Careful, it's got stickers on it.''

"Can I call you Daddy yet?'' she whispered in his ear.

"Not yet, but it won't be long,'' he whispered back. "Did your mother swallow the bait?''

"The bait?''

Oops. Still had some work to do on kid lingo. But he'd get it down, just like the rest he still had to learn. And this time he'd do it right. "Is your mama inside?''

"Uh-huh. She's still lookin' for her keys. I hid 'em in the garbage can."

"Good going, sweetheart. Now give me a high five and scoot over to that friend's house you said you could go to."

"How long am I 'sposed to play with Lizabeth?"

"Think her mom will let you stay till dinner?" Audrey assured him she did that "lots lately since Mama's such a grouch."

Greg was a little sorry to see Audrey take off. Now who was the one hiding behind a child, he asked himself wryly as he let himself in the unlocked door. He didn't want to scare Chris, but even less did he want the door slammed in his face.

Shutting it softly behind him, he knew a sweet thrill at the sound of her voice, cursing profusely from the direction of her bedroom.

Divine intervention? What better place for a showdown; an even better place to kiss and make up.

Deciding the flowers would meet a kinder fate after the kiss and make-up part, he placed them on the piano bench. And then, his gaze lifting to the wedding picture atop the upright, he did something extremely difficult, but necessary.

He laid the roses beside the picture. In their time apart he had come to realize many things, and this was a symbol of his acceptance of the whole of her life. Just as Chris would have to accept his for them to make a good life together.

Treading quietly to her open bedroom, he watched from the doorway, devouring the sight of her dressed in a chambray shirt and faded jeans. Chris had never looked so good to him, her hair a mess, barefoot and pregnant, banging shut a drawer and yelling, "Damn! Damn, where the hell are those keys?"

Greg dug into his pocket, and lifting his own, jangled them. They sounded like bells and he could only think one kiss from Chris and oh, how they would ring.

"Audrey, you found them!" she said, whirling around. The smile on her face froze. And then she fell back against the dresser. One hand clutching at it, her other went to her stomach. But as his gaze hungrily followed the movement, she quickly jerked her palm from her belly.

"Audrey's gone to play so her mother and I can put our games away." He shut the door and locked it. "Hello, Chris."

CHAPTER TWENTY-FOUR

HELLO, HELLO, HELLO. There was an echo in her ears and it swept through her head, carrying the sound of the voice that haunted her dreams and her days.

"God, you look good to me," he said, walking slowly toward her while she commanded herself to run, to hide, to do anything but grab her scissors and stab him in his heart if he had one. Or worse, rush into his arms and cover his face with kisses.

She had no idea what she was going to say until she said it. "You look like hell yourself. Make that more like a tomcat who's spent too many nights on the prowl. Man can't live on sex alone, Greg."

He stopped short. Only several feet separated them but the heat of flaring emotions ran a mile wide and just as deep.

A flash of disbelief, then anger crossed his face. But he quickly subdued both as if determined to stay cool in a volatile situation. Too bad, Chris decided. Her hormones were on a rampage and she wanted to vent the manic fury of each one on the man responsible.

"I'm afraid I don't understand where you've gotten such a wrong idea," he said evenly. "The only woman I've been hungry for is you and I'm beyond starved. There hasn't been anyone else, Chris." He glanced at her stomach and she instinctively covered it. "I won't ask if the same holds true for you."

No one else for him? *Yeah, right.* The last thing she wanted to endure were more professions of innocence, lies she was desperate to hear. And wanting to hear them made her more furious than ever, flush with the need to lash out and hurt him as cruelly as he had her.

"Oh, but I do think you should ask," she said with a flippant little laugh. "I didn't waste any time taking your advice. And what good advice it was. But I'm afraid it backfired on you since it made me realize what we had together wasn't nearly as special as I had thought."

His eyes probed hers and she prayed he wouldn't see past her lie and into the longing she was frantic to suppress.

"I don't believe you."

"Then why don't you ask Jerry?"

Chris watched the clench of his jaw with enormous satisfaction. But then, suddenly, he reached for his belt and whipped it from his pants. With a savage flash of movement, he flung it across the room.

"What do you think you're doing?" she demanded, edging away from the dresser, her eyes darting around for the best path of escape.

"Short as your memory seems to be, I'm going to refresh it. Old friends that we are, indulge me with a comparative analysis once we're done. *Blow by blow.*"

"No!" Chris latched on to a vase behind her and hurled it at his nose, dead center. He caught the porcelain neatly and she heard it shatter against the floor as she raced just beyond his reach.

Seconds later, she felt the surprisingly gentle clamp of his grip around her waist. But there was nothing gentle in his grind against her buttocks nor in his tone.

"'No' won't get it, babe, any more than 'Stop.' The password is *roses* and I'll hear you scream it before I'm done with you. And then, *then,* I'm going to hear you say that you love me and Jerry was a mistake. I can forgive a mistake. But I can't forgive you wanting him and not me. And you won't want him after this. Believe me, it's true."

Knowing just how true it was, Chris struggled to break free. A real struggle, not a pretend one this time. She couldn't let him take her or her fate would be sealed. She'd let him use her again however he wanted while he snuck around behind her back and ultimately destroyed her.

The knee she jerked up to his groin he easily deflected, but her fingernails connected with his face and she was both repelled and riveted by the three thin streaks she raked, making blood bead to the surface of his cheek.

"Such a bad girl you are," he said with mocking approval as he gripped her wrists and efficiently bound them with his tie. "You just earned yourself a worse punishment."

The baby. If he was too rough she might suffer the miscarriage she had prayed for and had come to thank

God heaven had refused to give. But, should she plead to be spared for the baby's sake, Greg would use their child against her to get whatever he wanted.

Grasping at straws, she said, "Go ahead, Greg. Go ahead and do whatever you want. Just be prepared to get slapped with a lawsuit. I'll cry 'Rape' before I cry 'Roses.'"

"Rape?" He laughed a single harsh laugh. "No way, babe. I'm going to make you wet and I'm going to make you beg. For me, Chris, only for me. You're going to open your legs wide, wrap them around mine, and take me home. We're picking up where we left off. As in *now*."

Chris knew there was no escaping the inevitable; he was bent on it and she was no match for his strength. The best she could do would be to cut off her feelings by remembering the woman's voice and remain silent.

And so, she retaliated with indifference—a weapon more powerful than hate. She went still, stood there and let him take off her clothes. No assistance, no resistance. She could have been a pliable statue, movable but cold.

Shutting her eyes, she refused to look at him; made no reply to his alternately sweet and dirty words. But as she allowed him to carry her stiff form to the bed and endured his languorous stroking, she realized his punishment was immeasurably worse than had he taken her by force.

Gentleness. Tenderness beyond belief. Kisses to her closed eyes, kisses to her breasts, kisses and more kisses to her stomach. She felt loved, treasured, her body worshiped. Her body cared not at all that he had betrayed her. And her heart joined in the conspiracy, whispering that no man could touch a woman like this and be capable of betrayal.

It was heaven. It was hell. She was coming undone, her defenses unraveling, her legs spreading wide, hips rising, moans breaking from her throat amid whimpers of "Greg, please, please, hold me. Be inside me where you belong."

When she beseeched him with raised hands, he untied her wrists and she traced his beloved face, swept her palms over his back and urged him closer, closer.

How carefully he lowered himself over her; how restrained was his entry when so easily he could have thrust and met an eager acceptance. Buried inside her, he remained there, unmoving, pressed firm against her womb, their baby.

Their baby. It was then that Chris began to cry.

Licking at her tears, he murmured, "I love you blind, Chris. I'm so blind with it, I don't care whose baby it is if you'll let me raise it as mine."

Her shock was ample to halt her tears. Staring at him, unblinking, she saw the truth of his words in his gaze and knew for a certainty that no woman had ever been loved more than this man loved her.

"How—how did you find out?"

"From the mouths of babes—the other one that I want as much as the child you're carrying."

And he didn't even care if it was his. Her head was spinning, her heart rose and flew on a wing. What more proof of commitment did she need? But that other woman…there *had* to be an explanation, just had to be. One she should have asked for instead of jumping to conclusions without giving him a chance.

No more repeating mistakes. No more shutting him out or letting lies or pride, reason or fear come between them.

Suddenly needful to assure him, to share this miracle of theirs, she said with a tremulous smile, "There was no other man, Greg. The baby is yours."

Forever would she remember the light in his eyes, the slow spread of his grin, the way he threw back his head and shouted, *"Yes!"*

They made love and never would she forget that, either. It was filled with passion and a sweeping tenderness, soft laughter and pregnant tears. He cried some, too. And never had Greg seemed so strong to her as when he shed them openly, his tears of joy and relief mingling with the blood she had drawn.

Their lovemaking was healing, binding, and in the aftermath when he said solemnly, "Marry me," she didn't have to think twice about her answer.

"Yes, yes," she chanted.

"And it's yes because you love me."

"I love you enough to be more afraid of losing you to someone else than to death. I love you enough to hate you just as much. And when you came here, I hated you enough to lie." She told him about the call and though she had trouble understanding the unique friendship he had with his ex-wife, she could understand how any woman would prize him enough to keep him any way she could. Eileen was no threat and that made it easier to accept Greg's wish to remain friends with her. He even suggested that Chris would come to like her, too.

And maybe she would. After all, Eileen had offered temptation when Greg had been vulnerable for that comfort and his refusal had proved something to them both.

Wanting no secrets between them, Chris recounted her ordeal at the clinic, the reasons that had driven her there.

He listened patiently and there was a wealth of sympathy in his gaze, while his stroking of her belly showed a protectiveness to rival that which had reversed her decision.

"In the end, I couldn't do it. I just—just couldn't let the baby go."

"Thank God for that," he said, his gaze lifting to heaven and then lowering to her. "What stopped you?"

"At the time, I wasn't sure. It was an instinctive thing, not based on reason at all. But then, just like it was after I cut us off and realized I'd made the mistake of my life, I did some sorting and came up with the real reason." Tracing the red streaks she had inflicted with the intensity of passion only Greg had ever roused in her, Chris knew how very true the reason was.

"I wanted to believe it was simply my moral fiber and maternal instincts that stopped me," she confessed. "Only, that wasn't true. Had it been another man's child, I might have gone through with it. But the baby was yours. I wanted your baby, Greg. And I wanted to see you in it, so I could always remember what it was like to come alive, to feel all the horrible, wonderful things you made me feel that I was sure were gone forever.''

"'Forever' is here," he told her, though she needed no assurance it was true. "Our bond is solid, Chris. We've got what it takes to get us through, no matter what. Our love, it's tough enough to last.''

"A trial by fire," she whispered. "If we survived this, we can survive anything.''

"Even Arlene." He laughed ruefully. "You are marrying me for better or for worse, and worse is due to spend the summer with us. I...I've decided I'm not ready to cut my losses with her. Better late than never, I want to try to make a difference in her life if I can. I'm going to need your help, Chris.''

"Hey," she said, knuckling his jaw, "what are wives for? We'll take Arlene on together, Greg.''

The sound of a light knock at the bedroom door brought them both upright.

"Oh dear," she groaned. "Reality intrudes. I hope you realize kids have a knack for terrible timing.''

"Actually, Audrey's timing is perfect." A quick kiss and he called out, "We'll be there in a minute, sweetheart. Your mom and your soon-to-be daddy are just about through talking.''

A whoop of delight, a "Yea! Yea! Yea! Daddy, you did it!" accompanied the sound of excited jumping on the other side of the door. They made it a game of who could get dressed the fastest, but as Greg raced Chris for first dibs on hugs, she stopped him short.

"Your face. Let me tend it first."

"Tend it later. Here." He pulled out a handkerchief and said, "Spit. You know, the way moms do while their kids go 'Yuck.'" But as Chris followed orders, he winked and said, "Yum."

Audrey was waiting, still hopping almost high enough to touch the clouds, when they came to her, arm in arm.

Greg bent down and said formally, "I have a very important question to put to you and your mother."

"What happened to your face?"

"I, uh…borrowed your mother's leg shaver for my whiskers and had a little accident. Want to kiss it and make it all better?"

She did, then patted his cheek. "All better?"

Better? Sweet heaven, Greg thought, life didn't get any better than this. He pulled out two ring boxes from his pocket but left the mitten he would forever treasure. "You made it so good, Audrey, that I'm proposing to you first."

Lifting the velvet top and then the tiny diamond ring inside, he held it over Audrey's right ring finger. "Your left hand is meant to be saved for a man who'll have to ask me for it and promise to be as good to you as I promise to be to your mother. Audrey Nicholson, will you be my daughter?"

At her eager nod, he slipped the ring down her finger, then kissed it.

"Mama's turn now," she said, holding up her hand and admiring the diamond just before she licked it.

Greg stood, pulled Audrey next to him, and felt his heart expand until he thought it would burst.

"You said 'Yes' already, but I'd like to hear it again while I put this on." He took her gasp as a definite yes and slipped on the damn gaudiest diamond he'd been able to find in the jewelry store; a rock as big and solid as he felt with Chris by his side.

"Chris Nicholson, seeing that your daughter's agreed to be mine, I'm in big trouble if you're not equally agreeable. Say you'll be my wife. Again. And again and..."

Chris not only said it, she confirmed her promise with an unending kiss that didn't let up until Audrey tugged at his arm and said, "You forgot to give Mama these."

Greg took the roses and extended them like the vow they were to Chris.

"Roses," he whispered. "I give you roses."

"And I share them with you," she said, clasping her hands over his. The scent of roses lifted between them, surrounding them with sweetness.

"I'll never betray you, Chris."

"And I'll never betray you by doubting it. *Roses,* Greg. My trust in you is complete."

He laid the roses at Chris's feet, singing softly, "Yummy, yummy, yummy, she's got my love in her tummy." His palm moved there, and she laid her own hand over his. Then Audrey's joined theirs.

"And now we're gonna be a family," their daughter pronounced.

"That's right, sweetheart." His steady gaze meeting Chris's, he committed himself with a vow as sacred as their sex, as binding as their secret word. "And this family is for keeps."

Harlequin Romance®

Delightful

Affectionate

Romantic

Emotional

Tender

Original

Daring

Riveting

Enchanting

Adventurous

Moving

Harlequin Romance—the
series that has it all!

HARLEQUIN PRESENTS®

**The world's bestselling romance series...
The series that brings you your favorite authors,
month after month:**

Helen Bianchin...Emma Darcy
Lynne Graham...Penny Jordan
Miranda Lee...Sandra Morton
Anne Mather...Carole Mortimer
Susan Napier...Michelle Reid

and many more uniquely talented authors!

Wealthy, powerful, gorgeous men...
Women who have feelings just like your own...
The stories you love, set in exotic, glamorous locations...

HARLEQUIN PRESENTS,
Seduction and passion guaranteed!

Visit us at www.eHarlequin.com

HPGEN00

Harlequin® Historical

From rugged lawmen and
valiant knights to defiant heiresses
and spirited frontierswomen,
Harlequin Historicals will
capture your imagination with
their dramatic scope, passion
and adventure.

Harlequin Historicals…
they're too good to miss!

HHGENR

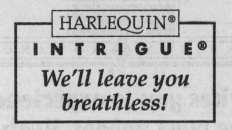